THE LAST SUMMER

Boris Pasternak had been recognized as a leading Russian poet many years before the famous *Doctor Zhivago* was published, but it was that book and his refusal of the Nobel Prize which made his name a household word in the West. He was born in Moscow in 1890, the eldest son of Leonid Pasternak, a painter, and Rose Kaufman-Pasternak, a musician. He had an exceptionally happy childhood and inherited from his mother a deep love of music which was his initial inspiration and the first medium of his creative efforts. During the First World War he worked in a factory in the Urals and after the revolution was employed in the library of the Commissariat for Education. He lived mostly in Moscow.

Pasternak translated Shakespeare, Verlaine, and several German writers (among them Goethe, Kleist, and Rilke) into Russian. His prose writings are few; *Doctor Zhivago* was his only full-length novel. He wrote short stories and two short autobiographical works, as well as a number of volumes of poetry. He died in the spring of 1960.

BORIS PASTERNAK

THE LAST SUMMER

TRANSLATED BY GEORGE REAVEY

*

WITH AN INTRODUCTION
BY
LYDIA SLATER

PENGUIN BOOKS

Penguin Books Ltd, Harmondsworth, Middlesex, England
Penguin Books, 625 Madison Avenue, New York, New York 10022, U.S.A.
Penguin Books Australia Ltd, Ringwood, Victoria, Australia
Penguin Books Canada Ltd, 2801 John Street, Markham, Ontario, Canada L3R 1B4
Penguin Books (N.Z.) Ltd, 182–190 Wairau Road, Auckland 10, New Zealand

—

Povest first published 1934
This translation first published by Peter Owen 1959
Revised translation published in Penguin Books 1960
Reprinted 1961, 1965, 1967, 1970, 1973, 1976, 1982

—

—

Set, printed and bound in Great Britain by
Cox & Wyman Ltd, Reading
Set in Monotype Bembo

INTRODUCTION
TO THE PENGUIN EDITION

WHEN, with the publication of *Doctor Zhivago* in the West, and more particularly after the award to Boris Pasternak of the Nobel Prize in October 1958, his name became a household word, and the hysterical sensation-mongers of East and West made him the centre of a violent and ugly political campaign, they completely misunderstood and misinterpreted his book and its message. True, there was enough genuine recognition and scholarly appreciation too, but it was constantly being drowned by the unbearable buzz of the loudest and cheapest of professional bluebottles, whose aim in life it is to convince their public of the myth that it appreciates only filth, money-talk, and scandal, and accordingly to feed it nothing else. How much all this hullaballoo must have hurt and astonished Pasternak is easy to understand if one remembers his own views on fame, on 'fireworks' and 'circus-smell', and, in contrast, on 'silence, best of sounds on earth'. I think that the following extracts sufficiently illustrate his attitude:

It is not seemly to be famous;
Celebrity does not exalt. . . .

To give your all – this is creation
And not – to deafen and eclipse.
How shameful, when you have no meaning
To be on everybody's lips. . . .

Into obscurity retiring
Try your development to hide,
As autumn mist on early mornings
Conceals the dreaming countryside.

Another, step by step, will follow
The living imprint of your feet,
But you yourself must not distinguish
Your victory from your defeat. . . .

How far removed is the pre-1958 Pasternak, in this modest, serious, and silent mood, from the whirlpool into which he was so soon to be drawn, and which made it impossible for him to continue in seclusion his conscientious and fruitful work. How foreign, in what direct contrast to his own feelings, were the sensation-mad antics of world journalism! – and yet, disgusting though they were and however much they may have turned one's stomach at the time, the harm they did was not permanent. Something more dangerous was happening in the meantime: publishers and translators all over the world got to work on every available scrap of Pasternak's writings in a feverish race to be the first to publish this or that item and to secure the copyright for it; a few of them, alas, were more concerned with the speed than with the quality of their publication, and though their motives were very understandable and only too human, there is no escaping the fact that for Pasternak himself this must have been a great disappointment and a disservice, for his original texts were often distorted beyond recognition. To do justice to the translators, it must be said that they were not only harassed by the pace set them by their rivals, but confronted with a very difficult and thankless task in the first place. Quite apart from the genuine complexity of Pasternak's language and the impossibility, for anyone but a true poet of his own magnitude, of rendering adequately the poetry even of his prose into a different language, it must have been utterly bewildering for a non-Russian who had no inborn feeling for the language to have to decide what particular meaning, out of many in the dictionary, the author had in mind when using this or that word in an unusually involved context; often several Russian words of seemingly the same root, and sounding almost alike, have completely different and sometimes even opposite meanings; how can any foreigner then be sure that he has happened to guess the right one? Time and again they failed. Thus it is indeed more surprising to find that some translations from Pasternak really do have something in common with the original text. And this, I think, is the case with George Reavey's translation of *The Last Summer*, in the form in which it is now presented.

The Last Summer (whose original title is simply *A Tale – Povest*) lies about half-way between *The Childhood of Luvers* and *Doctor Zhivago*, and has, in one way or another, connexions with both. Fifty years of creative life separate these last two works, and it is not only the years that divide them; they might have been written by two different people.

Doctor Zhivago was not written in one go, at the end of the fifties: Pasternak carried the unwritten book within him for many, many years, and its ideas and the characters in it grew and matured and changed, until some of them became very different from their prototypes – less tangible and more universal. I see *Doctor Zhivago* not as a homogeneous whole but as a magnificent composition made up of a multitude of integral components. It is a work of such complexity and concentration that it leaves one stunned and breathless after the first reading, and one has to read it again and again. The author appears now as the passionate philosopher, whose very passion compels him to write with 'unheard-of simplicity', now as the mature epic poet, now as the bard of Slavonic folk-lore, now as the Christian, and at times even as the youthful creator of Zhenia Luvers: it is he, I think, who is mainly responsible for the matchless descriptions of season, landscapes, and weather which are scattered throughout the book, and also for some of Zhivago's poems.

The Childhood of Luvers is in my opinion the most perfect piece of prose ever published by Pasternak. Its psychology and language stand comparison even with Tolstoy. Unfortunately it is only a

7

fragment of a larger novel, only the first few chapters of it. The rest, not only conceived but already written down, was lost in anti-German riots at the beginning of the First World War. I remember my brother reading parts of it to my parents when I was a child.

Many more manuscripts were lost in various circumstances in the course of his life, but Pasternak allegedly did not regret it; he says that

In life it is more necessary to lose than to gain. A seed will only germinate if it dies. One has to live without getting tired, one must look forward, and feed on one's living reserves, which oblivion no less than memory produces.

(See also the remaining stanzas of 'It is not seemly'.)

The Last Summer is set in the same part of Russia as *The Childhood of Luvers* – near a factory town in the Urals, on the banks of the Kama. Serezha, the hero, arrives there to visit his elder sister, married to a factory employee. Apart from the fictitious details of Serezha's own family and background, the story (and certainly the whole of Serezha's thoughts and personal recollections) are purely autobiographical. The characters who appear in Ousolie*
– Serezha's brother-in-law, a fussy and artificially simple man, who tries to play the fool, though he 'could be a natural fool without trying', the telephone-operator and dressmaker, the mysterious Lemokh, the workmen and the Tartars – all these, and particularly Serezha's elder sister, a former revolutionary, slightly irritating and somewhat comic, whom Pasternak introduces mainly in order to set off more distinctly Serezha's own character in the turmoil of formation: all these were drawn from life, from the milieu of friends and acquaintances and workmen in the chemical factories in the Urals, where Pasternak spent a couple of winters at the invitation of a friend, a remarkable man and scientist. Like,

* Ousolie and Solikamsk are salt-towns, bearing within their very names the salty whiteness of their appearance.

8

much later, his discovery of Georgia, his visit to the Urals must have been a tremendous experience and a revelation to Pasternak, and gave him inexhaustible material from which he could draw at will in the future. It is fascinating to read his account of a winter journey, in March 1917, from the 'Quiet Mountain' works to another factory, situated beyond 'the limitless snow desert of a vast frozen river'. Wrapped up in three *azyams*, unable to move, he lay like a heavy sack, in a mass of hay, sleeping, waking, and dozing for hours on end, at the bottom of a covered sledge drawn by three horses, one behind the other, racing among snowdrifts and through dense glittering forests. Every now and then the driver had to jump off and run alongside the sledge, supporting it with his shoulder to prevent it from overturning. Then, the changing of horses at night, in an encampment, reminiscent of tales about robbers; a dim light in the hut; the samovar is hissing, the clock ticks on; while the newly-arrived sledge-driver takes off his overcoat and warms himself, talking quietly to the woman who is preparing his supper, another driver wipes his moustache, buttons up his armyak, and goes out into the frost to harness a fresh team of horses. All this, exactly as in the days of Pugachev, two hundred years ago; and next to it, a most up-to-date chemical factory, amid the same endless snowy waste.

Many of Pasternak's earlier poems are the fruit of his experience of the Kama district and the Urals, and a number of his prose works abound in variations on the same theme. We get to know the Northern spring, slow and timid in its preparations, and then suddenly bursting all barriers and spreading like wildfire; the ice melting and breaking on the northern rivers – an event as majestic in its violence as any tropical thunderstorm; the description of Siberian sunsets and dawns, nightingales, waterfalls, mountains, and timber; a moonlit snowfield, and the plaintive baying of just-visible wolves, foreboding disaster; the sheer pleasure of cutting large, clean, glittering slices of blinding snow, in bright sunshine, while clearing a snowed-up railway-line – all these are unforgettable passages.

9

Pasternak loves train journeys, and loves describing them – though 'describing' is not the right word for what he does. These chapters, like the one in *The Last Summer*, are always immensely exciting, and absolutely true to life in each case, but I think that the summer journey that takes the Luvers family from Perm to Ekaterinburg over the Asian border is the most vivid and excitingly realistic of them all.

In *The Last Summer*, only the first few pages and the last three are concerned with life in Ousolie (but what jewels of laconic statement reveal here the images, the sounds and smells of the landscape!); the bulk of the story relates Serezha's recollections and ideas of the spring and summer of 1914. All this is Pasternak's own experience, though he does occasionally retoss and remould various situations and events. Thus we know that he 'spent about a year, in two separate stages . . . in the family of a rich businessman, Moritz Philipp, as tutor of their son Walter, a nice and affectionate boy'; and the Fresteln mansion and life there is a fairly exact replica of Pasternak's own experience.

However, the estate on the Oka river near Alexin and the military barges landing near it on the eve of mobilization, as related to Lemokh at the end of the book – all this has nothing to do with the Fresteln family: Pasternak describes this episode in more detail in his autobiography; he was then staying on the Baltrushaitis' estate as their son's temporary tutor, while also engaged in translating Kleist's *Der Zerbrochene Krug*. This came before the Philipp-Fresteln engagement.

I am tempted to quote here what Pasternak has to say about realism in art. He writes:

Realism would seem to consist not *of* a separate trend but *of* a special concentration in art, of a supreme degree of artistic precision . . . that decisive measure of creative detail which neither general aesthetic canons nor the contemporary public demand from the artist. It is at this very point that Romantic art is contented and stops short. . . . The realistic artist is quite differently placed.

His work is his cross and his destiny. For him there can be no indulging his fancy, no caprice. What time could he have for playthings, he, the plaything of his own destiny?

First of all, though, what is it that makes a man a realist? What forms him? I should say that it is an early impressionability in childhood and timely conscientiousness in manhood. It is just these two forces that impel him to take up work which the romantic artist neither sees nor has need of. It is his own memories which drive him on to the technical discoveries needed for their reproduction. Artistic realism as I understand it is the depth of the impression made on him by life, transformed into the main impetus of the artist, and forcing him to be inventive and original. . . . His work is original through and through, not because of his divergence from his contemporaries but because of the closeness to nature which was his model. It is always biographical, not out of egocentricity but because he sees his life as the means of knowing every life on earth.

The central theme of *The Last Summer* is poetry, the essence of which is the suffering woman. She is the leitmotif of most of Pasternak's work; but he is not the medieval knight with the name of his beloved on his banner, nor the more modern radical, fighting for the rights of women. His preoccupation with their suffering is on a different level. He writes of it in his reminiscences:

I shall not describe . . . how in the spring of 1901 a troop of Dahomeyan Amazons was on show at the Zoological Gardens. How for me the first sensation of woman was bound up with the sensation of a naked band, of closed ranks of misery, a tropical parade to the sound of a drum. How I became a slave to forms earlier than one should, because I saw in these women the form of slaves too soon. . . .

. . . From this intercourse with beggars and women pilgrims, from this neighbouring world of the world's spurned and rejected, and the things that happened to them, and their hysterical wailings on the nearby boulevards, I acquired much too early and retained for the rest of my life a feeling of terrifying and breathtaking pity for women.

It is impossible, in English, to feel sorry for someone without implying some sort of superiority on the part of the person who feels the pity. Not so in Russian, where to feel pity and to love someone are almost synonymous notions in popular usage (and expressed by the single word *zhalet*). Serezha feels *compassion* with the suffering women, he suffers – literally – with them and for them, and he loves the streetwalker Sashka in the same compassionate, non-carnal way as he loves Arild or Mary Queen of Scots, because he is a poet and because the suffering woman becomes his sister; because, in the words of one of the prostitutes, he was 'in some way like them' in his capacity of poet, of their suffering brother. Pasternak draws a parallel between the beautiful woman and the poet more explicitly and in a different way in his autobiography. He writes:

'Two expressions have long reached a common triviality: a genius and a beautiful woman. And how much they have in common!' 'From childhood a beautiful woman is inhibited in her movements', and God's nature 'is the only place where she can be quite herself, for with other people she cannot take a step without hurting others or herself being hurt'. 'She would like the night to notice her, the heart of the air to be wrung at the sight of her, the stars to find something to say of her.' But she would burst out laughing if such desires were ascribed to her. 'She is not thinking of anything like this. For thinking thoughts like these she has a distant brother in the world, who is fully accustomed to know her better than she knows herself and to be ultimately responsible for her.' 'She has a healthy liking for healthy nature and is unaware that reliance on the mutuality of the universe never leaves her.' She meets her lover and they walk on together. 'All at once the road widens somewhat and the place seems more solitary, so that they hope to rest a little and look about them; but often at this same time her distant brother makes his way into this place', they meet, and ' – whatever then may happen, no matter – a complete "I am you" binds them with all conceivable ties in the world, and proudly, youthfully, and wearily stamps the medal, profile upon profile'.

Serezha feels pity for Sashka and wants to help her, and to help all those other wretches; he dreams of some miraculous way to get hold of millions which he would distribute among them, to renew the universe, though he knows in his heart that it would not help and that there is no salvation. He muses on Sashka's childhood in the slums, at the railway crossing, and how she looks at the frightening engine-smoke, while a book is being written about her, called 'Childhood of a Woman'. But no, the book is not about her; it is about someone else: 'the name is not Russian and the town is different'. Was it about Lara Guichard? Or was it the childhood of Zhenia Luvers? But these two are worlds apart! Their only connexion is their suffering, for Zhenia too, without yet knowing it, is suffering for becoming a woman. The chapter is simply called 'The Long Days'. Or was that book written about Anna Tornskjold? One cannot help feeling that Anna's personality, though probably real, is not very important for the story. Serezha fell in love with her because she happened to be there. He needed her and his love for her as a driving force, as fuel for his poetry, for his thoughts and his feelings.

There is not much of a plot in *The Last Summer*; Pasternak is not really interested in plots. It is, in the words of V. S. Pritchett, a 'concerto in prose' – reminiscences loosely interwoven, cutting into each other, brilliant descriptions of people, situations, thunderstorms, and thoughts. Serezha writes the outline of his future drama, he writes it with such inspiration, and it carries him away so far (as it does the reader) that he forgets all about Anna and his love, and even her physical presence in the room behind him does not bring him out of his trance. He writes about himself and his music and his poetry, about birches and thunder and waterfalls and whirling leaves, and about the miraculous millions which he would not touch for himself. (And as I write this, I am struck by the strangeness of the coincidence – that Fate did, at the end of his life, give Pasternak just these abstract and miraculous millions which he could not and would not touch – a coincidence as absurd and seemingly impossible as those which abound in *Doctor Zhivago* and which reasonable people refuse to accept.)

The whole of the story of Mr Y is pure and undiluted poetry, at any rate in the original Russian. These passages are charged with such drama and lyricism that I cannot read them without tears.

In spite of the comical touch introduced by the arrival of the furious Mrs Fresteln, we cannot forget the mood of this drama and the sadness of its concluding words. For some reason, they remind me of a chapter in *Safe Conduct*, on 'that eternally recurring strangeness which may be called the poet's last year': it deals with the problems of ugly ducklings and similar questions, and is a quiet and seemingly ordinary, matter-of-fact discussion; but it leads one inescapably to the final truth, tentatively delayed by a last shred of hope, contained in a question-mark: 'But can there be such sadness when there is such joy? Is this not the second birth then? Is this death?'

With all his vitality and joy of living, his unconcern, and his humour, Pasternak bore within him an immense and unallayed sadness all his life. But perhaps, without this ever-present, though often unnoticed, sadness, his poetry in verse and prose would not have been the blessing and miracle it is.

Oxford, 1960   LYDIA SLATER

For references and quotations I have consulted the original Russian texts, where available, and also the following publications in English:

Doctor Zhivago, translated by M. Hayward and M. Harari. Collins and Harvill Press, 1958.

The Last Summer, translated by G. Reavey. Avon Books, 1959.

Fifty Poems, translated by L. Slater. ('It is not seemly' was first published in *The Times Literary Supplement*.) Allen & Unwin, 1963.*

The Collected Prose Works, translated by Beatrice Scott and Robert Payne. Lindsay Drummond (S. Shimanski), 1945.

Safe Conduct and Other Works, translated by Alec Brown. Elek Books, 1959.

I Remember, translated by David Magarshack. Pantheon and Collins, 1959.

An Essay in Autobiography, translated by M. Harari. Collins and Harvill Press, 1959.

Chopin (on the 135th anniversary of his birth), translated by Richard Newnham from a version revised by the author in 1959.

* *Fifty Poems* incorporates all my translations of Pasternak's poetry, including the collections published by Peter Russell in 1958 and 1959.—L.S.

THE LAST SUMMER

I

... that last summer when life still appeared to pay heed to individuals, and when it was easier and more natural to love than to hate.

AT the beginning of 1916, Serezha came to stay with his sister, Natasha, in Solikamsk. For the past ten years the scattered fragments of this tale have kept coming into my mind, and in the early days of the Revolution some portions of it found their way into print.

But the reader had better forget about these earlier versions or he will become confused as to what fate ultimately befell each character. I have changed the names of a number of these characters; as to the fates themselves, I shall leave them as I had found them in those years in the snow under the trees; and there will be no difference of opinion between my novel in verse, *Spectorsky*,* which I wrote at a later date, and this prose offering: the life in both of them is the same.

To be exact, Serezha arrived not in Solikamsk, but in Ousolie. A white pile, it glowed on the opposite bank of the river; and from the factory shore, from the kitchen of the doctor's freshly painted apartment, one could easily grasp on the very first day of arrival the why, wherefore and the purpose of the town. The sheer commercial

* *Spectorsky* – a narrative poem published in 1932.

masonry of the cathedral and the official buildings glimmered and grazed, dispersed by the blasting munitions of satiety, the powder of plenty. Reducing to neat squares this spectacle on the other bank – the handiwork of Ivan the Terrible and the Stroganovs, the doctor's windows shone brightly as though the fresh oil paint had been stirred and, in bags of creamy scum, spread over their wooden frames in honour of that distant perspective. Indeed, that must have been so – for the scant cracked palisades of the counting-house district had nothing to contribute.

In the bushes, to assist the ravens, a thaw was picking and pecking. Solitary sounds brooded over the water of black puddles under the snow. The whistling of a shunted locomotive at Veretie alternated with the shouts of playing children. The thud and hack of hatchets on the site of the nearest construction plant distracted one from listening to the vague organ-like shuffling of the distant factory. This could be more easily imagined – suggested by the sight of its five smoking caps – than actually heard. Horses neighed, dogs barked. The abruptly interrupted crowing of a raucous cockerel quivered like a tiny splinter on a thread. And from a distant tributary, where the drowsy whiskers of swaddled willow-bushes bristled from the snowdrifts, came the provocative staccato beat of a dynamo. The sounds were scant and they seemed drunken because they rolled in ruts. Between them, the muted sentences of the wintry plain unfurled, solemn and rakish. Somewhere in the vicinity and, according to local tradition, almost in the neighbouring village, the plain hid the foothills of the Urals. The plain had concealed them like deserters.

Serezha bumped into his sister at the door. Natasha was

about to leave the house on some household errand. Behind her stood a snout-faced girl in an unevenly-fastened short fur-lined coat. Natasha threw her shopping bag down on the window-sill and, while brother and sister embraced and chattered, the girl, snatching up Serezha's suitcase, dashed like a whirlwind, in her loose shuffling felt boots, into the interior of the apartment and just managed, at full tilt, like a craning speeding hoop, to avoid crashing into the dining-room table. Very soon, beneath a shower of questions, Serezha began awkwardly and unaccustomedly to wash away with Kazan soap the grimy traces of his sleepless last forty-eight hours; and, as he stood there with a towel over his shoulder, his sister noticed that he had grown both taller and thinner. Then he shaved. Kalyazin the brother-in-law, was away at work, and his razor with all its accessories, which Natasha fetched from the bed-room, rather daunted Serezha. The bright dining-room benevolently smelled of sausage. The fists of a thirteen-branched palm tree, fiercely pressed against the black lacquer of the piano, while the brass glare of the screwed-on candlesticks threatened, with its weight, to break the panel. Catching Serezha's glance, which slipped over the milky toilet tones of the oilcloth, Natasha said: 'We inherited all this from Pasha's predecessor. The furniture goes with the flat.' Then, hesitating, she added: 'I'd be terribly interested to hear what you think of the children. You know them only from photographs.'

The children were expected back from their walk any minute.

Serezha settled down to tea and, submitting to Natasha, explained to her that their mother's totally unexpected death had shaken him badly. He had been terrified of her dying that summer when, as he put it, she had really been at death's door, and he had gone to see her.

'Of course, just before your exams. They wrote and told me,' Natasha interposed.

'Ah, yes!' he picked up, almost choking. 'Indeed, I sat for those examinations! What it cost me to go through with them, and yet now it's as though a cloth had wiped all that time at the University from my mind.'

Continuing to knead the gummy pulp of the calatch and sipping from his glass, he told her how he had begun to prepare for the examinations in the spring, shortly after Natasha's visit to Moscow, but had had to drop everything as a result of their mother's illness, his trip to Petersburg and much else (here he again went over the list). But then, a month before the winter session, he had pulled himself together for work, but the regular distractions, which were an ingrained habit since childhood, were the hardest of all to overcome. He felt offended that, when he said 'one talent in the hand is worth ten in the bush', his sister failed to recognize the proverb which their deceased father had put into circulation among the family with special reference to him.

'Well, what then?' Natasha asked, hastening to cover up the awkwardness.

'How – what then? I forced the pace day and night, that's all.' And he tried to convince her that no delight could equal such a race, which he incidentally defined as *the exaltation of no leisure*. According to him, only this mental sport had helped him to master his inborn temptations, the chief of which was music, shelved since then.

And to prevent his sister interjecting anything, he informed her rapidly and without any apparent transition that Moscow had been in the fever of a building boom when the war broke out, and that the work had at first been continued, but had now been stopped in places with the result that many houses would never be completed.

'Why never?' she protested. 'Don't you have any hope that the war will end?'

But he kept silent, assuming that here, as everywhere else, talk of war, that is, of their total inability to conceive peace, would be a frequent topic, and that Kalyazin very likely was the chief spouter in this domain.

Suddenly Natasha was forcibly struck by the unhealthy anticipation with which Serezha ever more frequently and successfully had begun to ward off her curiosity. Then she realized that he was exhausted and, unconsciously trying to save herself from this mind-reading, suggested that he undress and go to sleep. But there was an unexpected interruption. A bell tinkled faintly. Assuming it was the children at the door, Serezha made a move to follow his sister, but, waving him away and muttering something, Natasha vanished into the bedroom. Serezha walked to the window and, placing his hands behind his back, stared into space.

In his state of exalted vagueness, he failed to catch the fury that was unleashed next door. Using every ounce of energy as she clutched the receiver, Natasha hammered some sort of pleasantries into those same spaces which spread before her brother's gaze. In the direction of the endless paling, which stretched at the far end of the village, a man was walking away with measured, heavy step, a man notable only for the fact that there was not a soul near him and that no one crossed his path. Mechanically observing the departing figure, Serezha saw in his mind's eye a wooded section of the countryside through which he had recently travelled. He saw the station, the empty buffet improvised from a board propped on trestles, the hills beyond the semaphor and the passengers, strolling, running madly and shoving, on that snow-heaped mound which separated the chilly railway carriages from the hot pies. By this time, the striding man had passed the paling and, turning behind it, had vanished from sight.

In the meantime, changes had been going on in the bedroom. The screaming over the telephone had ceased. Coughing with relief, Natasha was now inquiring how soon her blouse would be ready and was explaining how it should be sewn.

'Did you guess who it was?' she asked, entering and catching her brother's attentive scrutiny. 'That was Lemokh. He's here on factory business and he'll spend the evening with us.'

'What Lemokh? Why do you always scream?' Serezha interrupted her in a low voice. 'You might have warned me. When one chatters idly, imagining oneself to be alone in the flat, and someone is working next door, it is naturally upsetting. You should have told me you had the dressmaker there.'

At first the misunderstanding assumed some proportions but was then fully resolved. It turned out that there had been no one else in the bedroom; and that, when Natasha had been cut off from her even more distant connexion, she had continued chatting with the telephone operator, who had severed the connexion and who was sitting in a distant office at the other end of the village.

'A charming girl,' Natasha added. 'She's a dressmaker, too: she can't manage on her wages. She's also coming tonight. But that's uncertain, for she has a visitor from the front.'

'Do you know,' Serezha suddenly declared, 'I think I'll really go and lie down.'

'That's good,' his sister quickly agreed and led him into the room which had been prepared for him on the receipt of his letter. 'I'm amazed they discharged you,' she remarked on the way, glancing sideways at her brother. 'You're not limping at all.'

'Yes, just imagine it, no complications, by unanimous decision of the board. What are you doing?' he cried out, noticing that his sister was about to spread some sheets and was pulling off the bed cover. 'Leave it there. I'll lie down as I am. It's not necessary.'

'Well, as you wish.' She yielded and, glancing round the room like a housewife, said on the threshold: 'Sleep your fill and don't worry. I'll see to it that they don't make any noise; if you oversleep, we'll dine without you and your meal will be warmed up later. But to have forgotten Lemokh, that is unpardonable; he is a very very interesting man, a worthy man, and he has referred to you very warmly and correctly.'

'But what am I to do?' Serezha pleaded. 'I have never seen him, and I've just heard of him for the first time.'

He thought that even the door closed after his sister in a mildly reproachful way.

He undid his braces and, sitting down on the bed, began to unlace his boots.

*

Serezha's train had also brought to Veretie a sailor who was on shore leave from the torpedo boat *Novik*. His name was Fardybassov. From the station he had carried his small trunk direct to the office, kissed a woman relative of his who was employed there and at once, crushing the ice and splashing water, strode with long steps towards the Mechanical Workshop. Here, his arrival created a sensation. However, failing to discover in the crowd pressing round him the man he was seeking and learning that Otryganiev was now working in one of the new and recently constructed workshops, he set off at the same pace toward the Second Auxiliary, which he soon discovered behind the storehouse fences, at the fork of the narrow-gauge railway. The track crawled like a nasty little hem along the edge of a steep slope and frightened one by its obvious defencelessness, for on the forest verge a sentinel armed with a rifle paced up and down. Abandoning the road, Fardybassov ran down the field, scurrying from hillock to hillock and disappearing in stagnant ditches of summer's making. Then he climbed the height, where stood the wooden barracks which differed from an ordinary shed only because it frequently threw puffs of steam, like snowballs, at the silence reigning here.

'Otryganiev!' The sailor on leave grunted, after running up the steps and banging the door post with the palm of his hand. 'Otryganiev!' he grunted again into the depths of the structure where several peasants were dragging some sacks from place to place and a formidable motor, its flywheel seemingly immoblized in its lightning flight, raged and roared, protected from the open fields, as with a loose cover, by nothing but these weatherboards. Beneath it, the mad lever of the connecting-rod ground its pistons and squatted, sank through the floor and jerked back its sprained leg, terrorizing the whole of this structure with its St Vitus's dance.

'What juice are you pumping here?' the new arrival asked at once, by way of greeting a lame sluggard, who rose up in the doorway after hobbling forward from the machine on a withered leg.

'Yeremka!' This type had just time to fire back when he was at once seized by an attack of bitter, large-crumbed, *mahorka* coughing. 'Chloroform,' he pronounced in a voice drink-sodden to the point of tuberculosis, and then merely waved his hand as he experienced a renewed paroxysm of rattling in his throat.

'Tar-mixers, that's what you are!' the sailor exclaimed affectionately, waiting for the attack to die away.

But it never came to an end because, at this moment, two of the Tartars, detaching themselves from the rest, quickly climbed up a wall ladder and, from above, began to pour lime into the mixer, which produced an incredible din and wrapped the interior in white curling, sundering dust. In this cloud, Fardybassov began to yell out that the clerk had devoured his time, his days were counted – and thereupon he began to urge his friend to go hunting for the whole period of his leave. For this he had made his way here through the open country from the station.

After a certain lapse of time, spent in affectionate jeering at the apprentices, those who were awaiting their call-up, and the factories engaged in war work, Fardybassov, when finally about to leave, related how not so long ago, just

27

before Christmas, he had been blown up on a German minefield one night when sailing out of the Finnish Gulf; but all this was lies and sheer bravado as far as the characters were concerned, for Fardybassov was on board the *Novik*, whereas it was another torpedo boat of the flotilla that had trained its guns, dug the deep, and gone down, winding round itself a watery noose of savage depth and tightness.

*

Dusk was falling; there was frost in the air; water was being carried into the kitchen. The children came in and were shooed away. Now and then, Natasha would steal to the door. But Serezha could not sleep: he was only pretending to be asleep. Outside, the whole house was moving through the twilight into the evening. To the material slave-song of the floors and buckets, Serezha was thinking how unrecognizable everything would become in the light when all this movement was over. He would feel as if he had arrived a second time and, what was more important, well rested into the bargain. And the foretaste of novelty, which the lamps had already to some extent created, seethed and rumbled, passing from incarnation to incarnation. It inquired in childish voices where uncle was and when he would depart again, and, taught to glare forbiddingly, it very emotionally chided the quite blameless cat Mashka. In a swarm of maternal admonitions, it darted about amid the vapour of soup, flapping its wings at aprons and plates. No protests saved it from being bundled up again by fussy and irritable hands and marched out for another walk, hurried through the door to avoid admitting the chill air into the house. And not so soon, much later that evening, it became embodied in Kalyazin's bass irruption and that of his cane and his deep galoshes, which, despite his ten years of married life, had never surrendered to any instruction.

To induce sleep, Serezha obstinately tried to picture some summer noon, the first that might turn up. He knew that, if such an image were to manifest itself and he could arrest it, the vision would seal his eyes and rush snoring to his feet and brain. But he lay there for a long time, holding the spectacle of hot July right in front of his nose like a book, yet sleep still declined to visit him. It so happened that it was the summer of 1914 which had crept up, and this upset all his calculations. It was impossible to gaze upon that summer, sucking in its soporific clarity through clouded eyes: instead, it made him think, and pass from one remembrance to another. For this reason, we too shall absent ourselves for a long time from this flat in Ousolie.

It was at Ousolie that Natasha had received her commissions, and with that list, made illegible by minute jottings and frequent erasures, she had scoured Moscow on her arrival there in the spring of 1913. She had then stopped at Serezha's; but now from the smell of the construction timber, from the hum of the surrounding calm and from the condition of the roads in the village he imagined that he could see the very persons whom his sister had tried to oblige, when she had absented herself for whole days from her room on Kislovka street. The factory staff lived in real amity as one family. Her trip in 1913 had even been officially sanctioned, the husband's mission having been entrusted to the wife. All this nonsense was made possible only because all the links in that abstract chain, which ended in travelling expenses, were human beings, generated without exception by those crowded conditions in which, as on a tiny island, they had to huddle with their diverse degrees of literacy in the midst of three thousand miles of – throughout illiterate – snows. Profiting by the occasion, the management had even invested Natasha with certain powers to negotiate on its behalf in order to clarify certain trifling misunderstandings, which could easily have been solved by correspondence; and this was the reason why Natasha had to frequent the Ilyinka, explaining these visitations in a very ambiguous manner. She enclosed these 'calls' in emphatically comic quotation marks, letting it be understood at the same time that these quotation marks enclosed matters of 'ministerial importance'. But in her free time, and especially in the evening, she visited her own and her husband's Moscow friends.

With them she went to theatres and concerts. As she did in the case of her visits to the Ilyinka office, she gave these amusements the appearance of business, but which did not admit of quotation marks. That was because an important past had formerly bound her to the people with whom she now shared her visits to the Moscow Art Theatre and the Korsh Theatre. This past, available at will to enthusiastic interpretations with each new sifting of old times, now remained the only evidence of their former relationship. They all met, strongly welded by its remoteness, for they were now practising different professions, some as doctors, others as engineers, and others again as lawyers. Those, who had failed to renew their temporarily interrupted studies, worked in the offices of *The Russian Word*.

They all had families, and all, with the exception of those who had gone into literature, had children. Not all of them, of course, resembled each other; and they lived, not in a hive, but scattered among different streets; and, when visiting one of them, Natasha walked from the Kislovksaya to the tram stop on the Vosdvizhenka, but, when on the way to another, she walked along the Gazetnaya, the Kamergersky and so forth, crossing streets each more crooked, sinewy and more rag-market than the last.

It must be said that, except for one occasion in Georgievsky street, where she had to call on friends before attending a benefit concert at which the works of Chekhov were to be recited and singers would appear, there had been no talk of the past during this trip of Natasha's. And even on this occasion, just as soon as Natasha had begun to indulge her memories after finding in her friend's toilette case a red tie of the period of 'Women's Higher Education', her friend, whom she had been urging to hurry, had finished dressing, and, turning their backs on the mirror where the resurrected images had begun to float, all three of them, including her friend's husband, rolled out into the green, glassy-chill air of a spring evening. They did not refer to the past, also because they believed in their heart that the Revolution would come again. By virtue of a self-deception permissible in our day too, they imagined that the Revolution would be staged again, like a once temporarily suspended and later revived drama with fixed roles, that is, with all of them playing their old parts. This illusion was all the more natural that, believing deeply in the universally popular nature of their ideals, they all held the opinion that it was necessary to test their own conviction on living people. Becoming convinced of the complete and, to a certain extent, environmental oddity of the Revolution from the standpoint of the average Russian outlook, they could justly be puzzled as to where fresh amateurs and devotees for such a specialized and subtle undertaking could emerge.

Like all of them, Natasha believed that the most demanding cause of her youth had merely been postponed and that, when the hour struck, it would not pass her by. This belief explained all the faults of Natasha's character. It explained her self-assurance, which was softened only by her complete ignorance of her defect. It also explained those traits of Natasha's aimless righteousness and all-forgiving understanding, which inwardly illuminated her with an inexhaustible light and which yet did not correspond with anything in particular.

She had heard from relations that something was happening to Serezha. She was aware of everything, beginning with the name of Serezha's flame, Olga, and ending with the fact that the latter was happily married to an engineer. She did not ask her brother any questions. Acting thus from conventional discretion, she, like a luminary, ascribed it to a special virtue of her caste. She did not question Serezha, but, breathing the awareness that his story should be submitted to that thoughtful and sensitive principle which she herself personified, she waited for him to break his silence and to open his heart to her of his own accord. She laid claim to his sudden confession, awaiting it with professional impatience; and who will laugh at her if he take into account that her brother's story had in it the element of free love, a dramatic clash with the conventional bonds of matrimony, and the right of a strong healthy feeling and, Heavens, almost the whole of Leonid Andreyev. In the meantime, bridled banality affected Serezha more violently than unbridled and sparking stupidity. And when once he could not contain himself, his sister interpreted his evasiveness in her own way and, from his reluctant omissions, deduced that everything had gone wrong between the lovers. Then her feeling of competence only grew stronger because now, to the above attractive inventory, was added what was to her the necessary element of drama. For, however remote her brother might have been to her as a result of his having been born five years and some months later than her generation, she had eyes in her head and she perceived unmistakably that Serezha had no inherent propensity for folly and mischief. And the word 'drama', which Natasha spread among her acquaintances, was the only one not borrowed from her brother's vocabulary.

2

A GREAT many things suddenly fell behind Serezha when, after successfully passing his last examination, he sallied into the street as if capless, and, overwhelmed by the event, gazed excitedly round him. A youthful izvoschik, whose raised boot had parted his caftan, was sitting sideways in the driver's seat, glancing an inch or two under his horse and wholly surrendering himself to the oblivious clarity of the March air, as he waited indifferently for a summons from any quarter of the spacious square. A soulless copy of his free and easy attitude, the grey piebald mare stood blinking in the shafts as if the very rumble of the cobbled streets had bodily carried it there and harnessed it under the shaft bow. Everything in the vicinity seemed to imitate the horse and driver. Studded with clean cobbles, the bulging pavement resembled a crested document bordered with kerb-stones and street-lamps. The houses stood raised in a vacant eve-of-spring vigil as on a resilient base of four rubber tyres. Serezha looked round. Behind a railing, a ponderous door hung idly and canicularly on one of the greyest and most dilapidated of façades – a door which had closed quietly upon his twelve years at school. At precisely that moment it had been immured, and now forever. Serezha walked home. A flat sundown of pinching chill unexpectedly broke upon Nikitskaya street. A frosty purple gripped the stones. Serezha felt too abashed to glance at the passers-by. Everything that had happened to him was written on his face, and his leaping smile, as expansive as all of Moscow life at this hour, dominated his features.

Next day he called on one of his friends who, because he taught in a girls' high school, knew what was going on in the others. That winter he had mentioned to Serezha the possibility of a post in the spring in a private high school on Basmannaya street, a post that would become available on the retirement of a teacher of literature and psychology.

Serezha could not bear school literature or psychology. Besides, he knew that he could never teach in a girls' high school because he would have to sweat too hard among the girls without any reason or profit to anyone. But, exhausted finally by all the excitement of the examinations, he was now relaxing, that is, he allowed the days and the hours to shift him about at will. It was as though someone had then broken a jar of pussy-willow jam at the approaches to the University and, wallowing with all the town in the bitter-furred berries, he had given himself up to the sway of their tough, leaden folds. In this mood, he wandered into one of the cross-streets of Plyuschikha where his teacher friend lodged in digs.

The rooms had barricaded themselves from the rest of the world with a vast coaching yard. A file of empty cabs ascended toward the evening sky like the backbone of some fabled and only just flayed vertebrate. Here, more strongly than in the street, could be felt the presence of a fresh expanse, naked and heartaching, and there was much dung and hay. There was in particular a great deal of that sweet greyness, on the waves of which Serezha had drifted here. And just as he had been swept into rooms of smoky chatter, propped from the outside by a three-armed street-lamp, so he was also rushed in the following day's twilight to the Basmannaya street and into a leaden conversation with the lady Principal, beneath which bristled the branchy creaking of a big neglected garden, full of private girls'-school earth, silvery-mouse-coloured, and in parts, already raked over.

Then suddenly, though it was difficult to say in whose honour, along one of those leaden turnings of the past week, he found himself living in a mansion, tutor to the son of the Fresteln family, and here he remained, shaking the lead from his feet. And that was not surprising. He was given board and lodging and, besides, a salary twice as large as a high school teacher's, a vast room with three windows next door to the classroom and the free use of his leisure when not busy with his pupil. He was given everything except the cloth mill of the Frestelns, for never in his life before had he found it so easy, in a soft hat (he had been given a large advance), after his tea and books, to descend from the marble halls straight into the newbaked heat of the sunny street which, with its parallel pavements, hurried slopingly towards the square lying in hiding round the corner. It was in the Samotekh district and, despite the unfrequented character of the neighbourhood, Serezha had two encounters during his first walk. The first was a young man, who was walking on the opposite side of the street and who had been present on that memorable evening at Baltz's. There were two brothers there, the elder an engineer, and the younger had told him that, on finishing the Commercial school, he must do his army service, but he was not sure whether to volunteer or wait for his call-up. Now he was wearing a volunteer's uniform, and the fact that he was in uniform embarrassed Serezha so much that he merely nodded to him without stopping or crossing the street. Nor did the volunteer stop either, because he had sensed Serezha's embarrassment from his side of the street. Moreover, Serezha did not know the brothers' family name, for they had not been introduced, and he only remembered the elder as a very self-assured and probably successful man, and the younger as more reserved and far nicer.

The other encounter occurred on the same side of the street. He bumped into a stout good natured man, an editor of one of the Petersburg journals. His name was Kovalenko. He knew Serezha's works and approved of them; and, besides, he intended with Serezha's help, and that of several other previously admired eccentrics, to renew his early literary efforts. About this pumping of energies and other such nonsense, he always spoke with an immutable smile. This smile was characteristic of him, because he seemed to detect comic situations everywhere, and this irony served to protect him from them. Avoiding Serezha's polite inquiries, he asked him what he was doing now, but, with the Fresteln mansion on the tip of his tongue, Serezha just bit it back in time and, lying quickly just in case, replied that he was engaged on a new story. And since Kovalenko was bound to question him about its theme, he at once began to compose it in his mind.

But Kovalenko failed to make this inquiry and, instead, arranged to meet Serezha in a month's time on his next trip to Moscow and, without stopping and while mumbling something about some friends in whose half-empty apartment he was staying, quickly scribbled their address on a piece of paper. Serezha took it without glancing at it and, folding it in four, thrust it into his waistcoat pocket. The ironic smile with which Kovalenko had done all this did not say anything to him because it was inseparable from Kovalenko.

Taking leave of his well-wisher, Serezha returned to the mansion by a roundabout way in order to avoid having to walk beside the man with whom he had terminated the conversation on such a final and natural note. Moreover, he was amazed at the whirlwind that was now blowing through his head. He failed to notice that it was not the wind, but the continuation of his imaginary story, which concluded with the gradual fading away of the encounter and all that had happened. Nor did he realize that its theme was his own thought-evoking impressionability; and his emotions had been also stirred by the fact that everything round him was so wonderful and that he had been so successful in his examinations, his job and everything else in the world.

*

His tutorship in the Fresteln family had coincided with a series of changes in the household. Some of the changes had taken place before Serezha arrived; others were still due to occur. Shortly before his arrival the husband and wife had brought their quarrelling to a final lifelong issue and had taken up residence on separate floors of the mansion. Mr Fresteln occupied half of the ground floor, across the entrance hall to the right of the nursery and Serezha's quarters. Mrs Fresteln spread herself over the entire top floor where, besides her three rooms and the drawing-room there was also a large ballroom with a Pompeian atrium and windows to both sides, and a dining-room with an adjacent serving-room.

Spring was early that year, and the noondays were warm and appetizing. At full steam, spring was rapidly forging ahead of the calendar and was inciting the household to prepare for the summer holidays. The Frestelns had an estate in the Tula province. Although up to the present the town mansion had been made draughty only by the airing being given to the trunks and suitcases on warm mornings, now the front door was already admitting ladies, the mothers of families, who wanted to rent some accommodation for the summer. The old hands were greeted like dear corpses miraculously restored to the bosom of the family, but with fresh candidates they discussed both the stone wings and the timber cottages and, on taking leave of them in the vestibule, insisted upon the special qualities of the Alexinsky air, which was remarkably nourishing, and the beauties of the Oka landscape, which could never be praised enough. And, incidentally all this was true.

In the courtyard carpets were being beaten, and clouds in tallow lumps hung over the garden, while puffs of irritating dust settling on a greasy sky, seemed to charge the air with imminent thunderstorms. But from the way in which the caretaker all covered in carpet dirt as with a network of hair, looked up at the sky, it was evident that there would be no rain. Lavrenty, the footman, in a lustring jacket instead of tails, and with a beater under his arm, passed through the vestibule into the yard. And watching all this, breathing in the odour of naphthaline and catching snatches of ladies' talk, Serezha could not help feeling that the mansion was already dressed for the journey and would at any moment dive underneath a tent of tremblingly moist, sultry-laurel birch-trees. In addition to all this, Mrs Fresteln's companion, without referring as yet to her dismissal, was preparing to go elsewhere and, seeking a new situation, absented herself even on working days. Her name was Anna Arild Tornskjold, but in the household, for the sake of brevity, she was called Mrs Arild. She was Danish, and always dressed in black, and it was depressing and strange to observe her in situations to which her duties exposed her.

She held herself precisely thus, in a spirit of oppressive isolation, crossing the hall diagonally with large strides and wearing a wide skirt, her hair done in a high knot, and, like an accomplice, she always smiled sympathetically at Serezha.

*

Thus, the day imperceptibly arrived when, adored by his pupil and on the friendliest of terms with the Frestelns – with regard to whom it was impossible to decide who was nicer because replacing in this way their broken ties, they indulged in backbiting privately with Serezha about each other – with a book in his hand and leaving his charge chasing a cat in the yard, Serezha walked from the yard into the garden. The garden paths were littered with fallen lilac, and only two or three bushes in the shade still bloomed to the end. Under these lilac bushes, with her elbows on the table and her head bent sideways, Mrs Arild was sitting and busily writing. A branch of ashy tedrahedrals, swaying slightly under its lilac load, tried in vain to peep over head at what she was writing. The writer blocked both the letter and correspondent from the whole world with the broad, thrice-wound knot of her light chestnut-fair hair. On the table mingled with some knitting lay a batch of opened letters. Across the sky swam slight clouds the colour of lilac and the note-paper. The sky itself, the colour of grey steel, cooled them. Catching the sound of steps, Mrs Arild first of all carefully blotted her letter, and then calmly raised her head. An iron garden chair stood next to her bench. Serezha dropped into it and, between them, the following conversation took place in German:

'I know Chekhov and Dostoyevsky,' Mrs Arild began, winding her arms round the back of the bench and looking

40

straight at Serezha. 'and I've been in Russia only five months. You're worse than the French. To believe in a woman's existence, you have to attribute to her some unpleasant secret. As though, in the lawful light she were something colourless like boiled water. But when she throws an obscene shadow on a screen, then it's another matter: you have no quarrel over that silhouette and think it beyond price. I have not yet seen the Russian countryside. But, in the cities, your weakness for shady alleys proves that you are not living your own life, and that each of you, in his own way, is straining to share someone else's. It's not that way in Denmark. Wait, I haven't finished . . . '

Here she turned away from Serezha and, observing a pile of fallen lilac on her letter, painstakingly blew it off. After a second, overcoming the pause, she continued:

'Last spring, in March, I lost my husband. He died a young man. He was only thirty-two. He was a clergyman.'

'But let me say,' Serezha interrupted her as he had planned, although he now wished to say something quite different, 'I have read Ibsen, but I did not understand you. You are in error. It's unjust to judge a whole country from the example of a single house.'

'Ah, so that's what you mean? You refer to the Frestelns? You must have a nice opinion of me. I am further from such mistakes than you, and I'll prove it to you at once. Did you guess that they were Jews and that they were concealing it from us?'

'What nonsense! Where did you hear that?'

'That's how observant you are! But I am convinced of it. And perhaps that is why I hate them so invincibly. But don't digress so much,' she began with renewed heat, without giving Serezha time to state that, on his father's side, this blood, so hateful to her, also flowed in his own veins, whereas there was no trace of it in the mansion; but instead of this, and according to his original plan, he managed to interject that all her ideas about sensuality were sheer Tolstoy: that is, the most Russian of all to deserve that name.

'That's not the point,' she cut in impatiently, hastening to break up the dispute and quickly moving to the edge of the bench nearer to Serezha. 'Listen!' she exclaimed vehemently, taking him by the hand. 'Your duty is to look after Harry, but I am sure that you are not obliged to wash him in the morning. Nor has it been suggested that you should massage the old man every day.'

This was so unexpected that Serezha dropped her hands.

'In Berlin this winter not a word was said about anything like that.' She continued, 'I went to the Hotel Adlon to discuss terms. I was to be employed as Mrs Fresteln's companion and not as her chambermaid, isn't that so? Here I am before you – a sane, reasonable person, you'll agree? Don't speak yet. The post was in a far land, in a strange country. And I agreed. Do you see how I was tricked? I don't know how Mrs Fresteln attracted me. I didn't size her up at first. And then all this developed, on the other side of the frontier, beyond Verzhbolov ... No, wait, I haven't finished. I had brought my husband to Berlin for an operation. He died in my arms, and I buried him there. I have no relatives. That's a lie. Yes, I have one, but another time about that. I was in a frightful state and without any means. And then suddenly there was this post. I read about it in a paper. And just accidentally, if you only knew!'

She moved to the middle of the bench, making a vague gesture with her hand at Serezha.

Mrs Fresteln passed through the glass gallery joining the kitchen to the mansion. The housekeeper followed her. Serezha at once repented that he had wrongly interpreted Mrs Arild's movement. She had no intention of hiding from anyone. On the contrary, having renewed the conversation with unnatural haste, she raised her voice and introduced into it a note of ironical disdain. But Mrs Fresteln did not hear her.

'You dine upstairs with her and Harry, and with the guests when they come. With my own ears I heard them say, in reply to your perplexity as to why I was not present at table, that I was ill. It is true that I often suffer from migraine. But, do you remember the day when, after the dessert, you were fooling about with Harry – please, don't nod so gaily! – the point is not that you have not forgotten about it, but that, when you ran into the serving-room, I almost died of shame. They explained to you that I myself had preferred to dine in a corner behind the door with the housekeeper (who really prefers that). But that's a trifle. Every morning I am obliged to attend to that quivering "treasure", like a child in the bath, to wrap sheets round her and then – to the point of exhaustion – rub her with cloths, brushes and pumice stone, and I don't know what else. And I can't tell you everything,' she unexpectedly concluded in a low voice and, taking a second breath as after a race, she wiped her scarlet face and turned it toward him.

43

Serezha remained silent and, from his martyred look, she guessed how deeply it had all affected him.

'Don't comfort me,' she begged, rising from the bench. 'But that is not what I wanted to say. I am reluctant to talk German. The minute you really deserve my confidence, I shall treat you differently. No, not in the Danish way. *We shall be friends, I'm sure.*'*

Having failed to warn her that he understood English, but had forgotten how to speak the little he knew, Serezha again said the wrong thing, answering *gut* rather than *well*. But Mrs Arild, continuing in English, reminded him warmly and plainly (later translating this more coldly into German) that he should not forget what she had told him about the screens and the shady alleys. That she was a Nordic and a religious woman who could not tolerate licence; that this was both a request and a warning, and that he should bear it in mind.

3

THE weather was stifling. Serezha, with the aid of a grammar, was refreshing his scant and neglected study of English. At dinner-time, he and Harry used to go upstairs to the ballroom where they kicked their heels while waiting for Mrs Fresteln to appear. Then they would follow her into the dining-room. Mrs Arild would often arrive in the ballroom five or ten minutes before Mrs Fresteln; and Serezha would talk loudly with the Danish woman until the lady of the house emerged and then part from her with

* In English in the original text.

44

obvious regret. The procession of three, headed by Mrs Fresteln, would then proceed to the dining-room and, the nearer they got to the door, the more the lady's companion was washed away to the left. Thus their ways parted.

For some time, Mrs Fresteln had been obliged to put up with the obstinacy with which Serezha insisted on referring to the main dining-room as the 'serving room', and the room next door, where they carved the chickens and served the ice cream, as the 'dining-room'. But she had grown to expect certain peculiarities from him, for she regarded him as an eccentric even though she did not always understand his jokes. She trusted the tutor and was not disappointed. He had no grudge against her even now, just as he bore no grudge against anyone. In a human being he could only hate his own antagonist, that is, a scornfully provoking and easy victory over life, one that had avoided all its most difficult and valuable elements. But the people, who could personify this possibility, were very rare.

After dinner, whole trays of smashed and broken harmonies slid downstairs. They rolled down and splintered in unexpected bursts, more abrupt and striking than any waiter's awkwardness. In between these turbulent falls, spread miles of carpeted silence. That was Arild upstairs, behind pairs of padded and tightly shut doors, playing Schuman and Chopin on the grand piano. At such moments, more involuntarily than usual, one had a desire to stare out of the window. But no changes were observable there: the sky was not moved by these outpourings. It continued to stand, like a sultry pillar, upon its fixed principle of rainlessness, while for forty miles round, beneath it, splashed a dead sea of dust, like a sacrificial fire simultaneously set alight from several ends by carters on the site of five good stations and in the centre of a brick desert beyond the Chinese wall of the city.

Everything was in confusion. The Frestelns stayed on in town, and Mrs Arild stayed too much in the mansion. But suddenly fate justified everything just when the incomprehensibility of their delayed departure had begun to surprise everyone. Harry fell ill with measles, and the move to the country estate was postponed until his recovery. The sandy whirlwinds did not diminish, rain was not in sight, and gradually everyone became accustomed to this. It even began to seem as if they were still living the same week-in-week-out stagnating day – a day which had not been hauled away in time to the police-station. So this day increased in strength and bullied everyone. And now, in the street, every dog knew it. But for the nights, which still breathed some spectral variety, one would have run for witnesses and sealed up the withered calendar.

The streets resembled wandering poppy beds with travelling plants. Dazed ashgrey shadows moved, with drooping heads, along softened footways. Only once, on a Sunday, did Serezha and Mrs Arild have energy enough, after plunging their heads in a washbasin, to burst out of town. They drove to Sokolniki. However, here likewise the same fiery air hovered above the ponds, with this difference, that, while the sultriness was not observable to the eye in town, here it was visible. A layer of mingled dust, mist and locomotive smoke, hung, like an office ruler, across the black wood and, of course, this efficient spectre was far more frightening than the simple sultriness of the streets.

Incidentally, this layer hung at such a distance from the water that the boats could freely slip beneath it; but, when the squealing young ladies changed from the stern to the oars, their young men, as they rose to let them by, caught their caps on this meaty scum. Near the edge of the pond the sunset fumed, hissing sourly. Its purple resembled a lump of pig iron, heated white hot and drowned in a bog. From the same shore, a slippery plaintively-resonant roar of frogs swam in bursting bubbles.

In the meantime, twilight was falling. Mrs Arild chattered in English, and Serezha made timely responses. Ever more quickly they wound their way through the labyrinth, which would bring them back to their starting-point and which, at the same time, was the shortest cut to the turnpike where the trams stopped. They differed sharply from the rest of the strollers. Of all the couples crowding the wood, this particular couple reacted with most anxiety to the fall of night, and tried to escape from it as if night were right on their heels. When they glanced back, they seemed to measure the speed of its pursuit. In front of them, on all the paths they trod, there sprung up, like a solid forest, something in the nature of the presence of an elder. This transformed them into children. They now seized each other's hands, now dropped them in confusion. At times they lost the conviction of their own voices. It seemed as if they were being thrown now into a loud whisper, now into a far off, space-cracked shout. In reality, nothing of the sort was observable: they pronounced their words normally. At times Anna grew lighter and more transparent than a tulip petal, while Serezha experienced a chest-heat like that of the glass of a burning lamp. She saw how he struggled against the hot sooty draught to prevent it from pulling her in. Silently they stared at each other's face, and then painfully tore apart, as one might a whole living creature, this dual smile distorted by a prayer for mercy. Here, too, Serezha heard the words to which he had long ago submitted.

Ever more quickly they wound through the labyrinth of ingenious paths and yet, at the same time, came nearer the turnpike, from where already sounded the muffled ringing of trams, which were escaping from the empty carts galloping in full pursuit after them the whole length of the Stromynka. The jingling tram cords did a precise jig in the illuminated glass. From them, as from a well, a cool breath was wafted. Very soon the extreme and dustiest section of the wood stepped off in clogs from the ground on to the paved roadway. They had entered the town.

'How great and indelible man's humiliation must have been,' Serezha thought, 'that, having identified in advance all accidents with the past, he has grown to demand an earth, fundamentally new and in no way resembling that on which he has been so hurt or defeated!'

*

In those days the idea of wealth began to preoccupy him for the first time. He was overpowered by the immediate necessity of procuring it. He would have given his mythical fortune to Arild and begged her to distribute it more widely, all of it – to women. He himself would have named several recipients. It would have been a fortune in millions, and those selected to receive some of the millions would have passed the wealth to new recipients, who, in their turn, would have continued the good work of distribution.

Harry was already convalescing, but Mrs Fresteln remained constantly at his side. A bed was still being made up for her in the classroom. Serezha was now in the habit of leaving the house in the evening and returning only at dawn. In the next room Mrs Fresteln kept turning in bed and coughing, and in every way let it be known that she was aware of his late hours. If she had asked him where he had come from, he would have told her without reflecting all the places where he had been. She sensed this and, guarding against the seriousness with which he would have replied and which she would have had to swallow as her duty, left him in peace. He returned from his absences with the same remote light in his eyes as from the outing to Sokolniki.

One after another, several women on different nights had swum to the street surface, raised by chance and attraction from non-existence. Three new tales of women took their place beside the story of Arild. It would be difficult to determine why these confessions had poured in upon Serezha. He did not go to confess these women, judging that to be beneath him. As if to explain the unaccountable trust which drew them toward him, one of them told him that he was in some way like them.

This was said by the most hardened and thickly powdered, the most promiscuous of them all, who to the end of her days was on most familiar terms with everyone, who urged on the izvoschik with unprintable plaints about 'feeling cold' and who, by all the thrusts of her hoarse beauty, levelled everything she touched. Her little room on the second floor of a sagging, ill-smelling five-windowed house in no way differed in appearance from any of the poorer middle-class lodgings. Her walls were hung with cheap linens to which she pinned photographs and paper flowers. A folding table was hunched between the windows, brushing both sills with its wings. Opposite, close to a partition that failed to reach the ceiling, stood an iron bed. And yet, for all its resemblance to a human dwelling, this place was its complete contradiction.

The floor-mats, when spread under the guest's feet with a rare show of obeisance, invited him not to stand on ceremony with the woman of the house and appeared ready themselves to set the example of how to treat her. A stranger's reasoning was their only master. Everything in the room seemed to exist wide open, profluently, as in a flood. Even the windows appeared to be turned, not outwardly, but inwardly from the outside. Washed by public notoriety as by an inundation, the household things, without respect and in disorder, floated upon the broad name of Sashka.

But neither did Sashka pay any tribute to them. Everything she undertook, she did in motion, like a big swell and in the same way, without rise or fall. Approximately in the same way as, all the time, she threw out her resilient arms while undressing and talking all the time, so afterwards at dawn, conversing and pressing with her belly against the wing of the table and knocking over the empty bottles, she gulped down her own and Serezha's dregs.

And approximately in the same way and to the same degree, while standing in a nightshirt with her back to Serezha and answering him over her shoulder, she, without shamelessness or shame, made water in the tin basin, which the same old woman who let them in had carried into the room. Not one of her movements could be foretold, and her cracked speech rose and fell at the bidding of the same hot jerky snore that knocked aside her locks and burnt in her quick hands. Her answer to fate lay in the very smoothness of her nimble movements. All human naturalness, screaming and blaspheming, was hoisted here, as on a rack, to the height of a misery observable from every side. It became the duty of the surroundings, when viewed from this level, to be inspired on the spot, and from the stir of one's own excitement one could detect how unanimously, in all haste, the universal expanses were being ringed with salvation posts. More pungently than all pungencies, it smelled here of the signal pungency of Christianity.

At the night's end, an invisible nudge from the outside made the partition shake. Her 'man' had stumbled into the entrance hall. His nose for a stranger's presence, which was his most assured income, did not betray him even when blind drunk. Stepping softly in his high boots, he collapsed behind the nearby partition as soon as he entered and without making a sound soon ceased to exist. His quiet couch probably stood back to back with the professional bed. Very likely it was an old chest. Hardly had he begun to snore when a rat struck at him from below with its quick, greedy chisel. But silence drifted over again. The snoring suddenly ceased; the rat grew alert; and the familiar draught ran through the room. Things on nails and clay recognized their master. The thief behind the partition was capable of everything they did not dare. Serezha jumped out of bed.

'Where are you going? He'll kill you!' Sashka croaked with her whole inside and, crawling on the bed, hung on to his sleeve. 'To show your fury is easy, but if you go – I'll get beaten up.'

But Serezha himself did not know where he was rushing. In any case, his was not the jealousy Sashka had fancied, though it was invading his heart no less passionately. And if any moving bait to make a horse run has ever been cast in front of man to outweigh his reason and ensure his eternal motion, then that bait must be this instinct. It was this jealousy that sometimes makes us jealous of women or of life to death, as to a mysterious rival, and compels us to strive to be free to have the liberty to free her of whom we are jealous. And here, of course, was the same pungent smell.

It was still very early. On the opposite side of the road-way, one could already guess at the folding sheets of the triple iron sections of the wide granary doorways. The dusty windows showed grey, filled to a quarter with round cobbles. The dawn lay on the Tverskoy-Yamskoy, as on a weighing machine, and the air looked like chaff that was constantly being winnowed by it. Sashka sat at the table. A blessed drowsiness made her dizzy and bore her along like water. She chattered without stopping, and her talk resembled a healthy drowsing animal.

'Ah, Guilty Ivanovna!' Serezha quietly repeated without listening to his own words.

He was sitting on the window sill. People were already walking the streets.

'You're no medic,' Sashka was saying, her side pressed against a board. She either slumped down with her cheek pillowed in her elbow or, straightening her arm, examined it slowly from the side, from the shoulder to the wrist, as though it were no arm but, rather, a long road or her very life, which she alone could see. – 'No, you're no medic,' she continued. 'Medics are different. I can't make you out, but it's different when one of them walks behind me – I can tell him with my tail. You're a teacher, that's sure? Well, that's it. I'm frightened to death of catching "the cold". But you're no medic, no use asking you. Listen, you aren't a Tartar, are you? Well, you must come to see me. Come in the daytime. You won't lose the address, will you?'

They were chatting in low tones. Sashka was either convulsed in fits of provocative bead-like laughter or overcome with spasms of yawning during which she also scratched herself. Insatiable like a child and as though recovering her lost dignity, she enjoyed this still hour which also made Sashka feel more human.

In the midst of their chatter, Sashka, having called Poland the Kingdom of Poland, and boastfully nodded in the direction of the wall where in a shining nest of other such photographs hung the glossy scarecrow of an amiable non-commissioned officer, thus revealed her earliest and most precious memory – the first cause no doubt of all that had followed. It was to him that her plump, outstretched arm, now lost in space, seemed to lead. But, perhaps, it was not him. Suddenly the dawn flared, like dry hay, and, like dry hay, burnt itself out at once. Flies started to crawl upon the bulging bubbly window-panes.

The street-lamps and the mist exchanged beastly yawns. All in scattered sparks, the day was kindled and woke. Serezha felt that he had never loved anyone as much as Sashka; and then, in his mind's eye, he saw – winding further away toward the cemeteries – the roadway spotted with meaty red patches; and the cobbles on the roadway are larger and more spaced out as they are at the city gates. Breaking away and departing, breaking away and departing – goods wagons, empty or filled with cattle, glide smoothly across this roadway. Then something like a crash occurs: the wagons stop moving, and from the background rises a severed section of the street. Those are the unloaded flat-wagons moving at the same pace, linked together, but now blocked from sight by the dense wall of people and carts at the crossing. Here is a world of nettles and chickweed, and of the smell of field-mice but for the smoke. And here, too, is snivelling Sashka, playfully fidgeting him with the humour of a six-year-old. Finally, last of all, and in a terrible puffing frenzy – as though questioning the bystanders whether they have seen the wagons go by – a black perspiring locomotive hurries past – backwards, backwards. Then the barrier is raised, the street flashes forward like an arrow and now, cutting into each other from the opposite direction, the loaded carts and human calculations start advancing. And then, right into the middle of the roadway the smoke of the locomotive flops down like a fibrous, thrice-tied sack – the warm stomach of a monster, perhaps that very offal that the poorer folk of the slums feed on. And Sashka stops talking and watches how frightening this smoke could be amid the tea and colonial goods, the sale of cigars and tobacco, and sheet iron, and the policemen, while somewhere at that time a book is being written about her eyes and heels, entitled *The Childhood of a Woman*. There is a smell of oats on the road which the sun, to the point of making one's head ache, has stamped in horse urine. So then, in the end, (he thinks, foreseeing her future) catching the 'cold' she so dreads, losing her eyes and heels, her nose and her reason, she will run in for a moment, before retiring to the hospital, and possibly also the grave, to get the book which, as she has been told, has already described all this, every aspect of it, and it is only too true: she has lived like a fool and, like a fool, she will die.

She is not allowed on the pavement – she is led by a detachment in the roadway, and now look at the whim she has got! Someone said it, and she, the fool, took it up. It's just ridiculous. The book was about someone else: the name is not Russian and the town is different. Whereas her own name is in the cop's cloth-bound braided notebook – there she is and you can read about her. Well, and (a momentary pressure on the filthy trigger) ta-tra-tra, ta-ta-ta – it's all one. And the cops look a little more human. They escort the trigger-happy girls, while the noble public holds its tongue on a safety catch.

'What's going on in your head?' Sashka asked. 'Look at some of the other women. Don't stare at me: I'm a lady compared with them. Now don't worry about the time or anything. Maybe, you'll say, people are asleep now. A lot you understand about the likes of us! Oh, you make me laugh, you'll kill me, ha-ha-ha! Come here in the day-time. Never mind *him*. Don't be scared of him, he's meek, if you don't rub him the wrong way. He'll go out when you come in; or he'll be just sleeping, as you can see, and you couldn't wake him if you tried. Why he's upset you, I don't understand. It would be a wonder if he turned nasty. Others have come and have taken no offence. Well-born gents like you. Well, I'm near ready, just got to powder myself, and I mustn't forget my bag. Here, hold it. Well, let's go. I'll walk with you as far as the Sadovaya. I'll not be lonely on my way back, that I know. Day or night, you've only to wink an eye – they just swim, just swim, into your arms. You're not going my way? Well, all right, goodbye then, but don't forget. I'll go alone – that'll draw the stallions. You won't lose my address, will you?'

*

The streets on an empty stomach were impetuously straight and surly. A lewd dove-coloured howl of empti-ness still swept their transient, unpeopled length. Infre-quently, one encountered some lean lonely cannibal. Far off, on the roadway, a galloping cab horse of good breed pounded along with its puffed-out pigeon chest. Serezha strode towards Samoteki and, within half a mile of the Triumphal Arch, imagined someone on the pavement whistling after Sashka and her playfully slowing down, as she debated whether the man would cross the street or she should do so. Though the day had barely begun, tangled threads of sultry heat, as nightmarish as crumbs in the beard of a corpse, hung already in the turmoil of the lime-trees. And Serezha felt feverish.

4

HE must make a fortune at once. But, of course, not by work. Wages were no victory, and there was no freedom without victory. And, if possible, without public notoriety, without the admixture of legend. In Galilee, too, the event had been local: it had begun at home, spread to the street and, finally, ended in the world. His fortune would be millions; and, if such a whirlwind should sweep over women's hands, making the round of even one of the Tverskoy-Yamskoys women, it would renew the universe. And there lay the need – in an earth made new from its foundations.

'The chief thing,' Serezha said to himself, 'is not that they should undress, but rather dress themselves; the chief thing is not that they should get money, but that they should distribute it. But, until my plan is fulfilled,' he cautioned himself (there was no plan really), 'I must get hold of another type of money, some two hundred or even a hundred-and-fifty roubles.' (Here Nyura Rumina rose in his consciousness, and Sashka; and Anna Arild Tornskjold was not the last to emerge.) These were small sums of quite a different significance. As a temporary measure, he might accept such sums even from an honest source. 'Ah, Raskolnikov, Raskolnikov!' Serezha muttered. 'But what had the old pawnbroker to do with it? The old pawnbroker – that was just another Sashka in her old age . . . But the problem is – how to get these few hundred even from an honest source? I'm already two months overdawn with the Frestelns, and have nothing left to sell.'

It was an early June day. They were already taking Harry out for walks. In the mansion preparations were resumed for the summer holidays. Mrs Arild was often away on her affairs, which Harry's illness had interrupted. Then she was offered a post with an army family in the Poltava government.

'*Not Suvoroff – the other,*'* Arild explained in a full voice on the stairs, too lazy to mount for the letters. '*I forget always.*'*

And Serezha reeled off a whole list of generals, from Kutuzov to Kuropatkin, before it turned out to be Skobeleff. '*Awful, I cannot repeat. How would you pronounce it?*'*

The terms of her new situation were profitable, but once again, for the nth time now, she had to put off her decision. The reason was this. She had hardly received the offer, when she fell ill; and the severity of her illness made everyone conclude that she had caught it from Harry. In the meantime, a temperature as high as in measles, which had put her to bed that very evening and which exceeded 104 degrees, fell precipitously next morning to below 97 degrees. All this proved a mystery which the doctor failed to solve, but it left the poor girl very weak. Now the effects of the attack began to wear off, and the mansion was again shaken once or twice by the thunders of *Aufschwung*, as in the days when Serezha had not even dreamt of Raskolnikov's dilemmas.

That morning, Mrs Fresteln took Harry to visit some friends in Klyasma, intending to spend the night there if the weather permitted and the opportunity presented itself. Mr Fresteln had likewise departed. Half the day passed as

* In English in the original text.

58

though the Frestelns were still at home. Lavrenty, to oblige, had offered to serve Serezha's meal downstairs, but he preferred not to change the established routine of the servants and, without noticing it, dined upstairs at the exact hour and even in his appointed place, second to the right.

It was past four in the afternoon, and the Frestelns were still away. Serezha thought, in turn, of the millions and the two hundred roubles, and, thus engrossed, paced the room. Then suddenly he experienced a moment of such acute awareness that, forgetting everything else, he froze to the spot and became distraught and alert. But he could detect absolutely nothing. Only the room, flooded with sunshine, seemed barer and more spacious than before. He could resume his interrupted preoccupation. Yet, he did not. He had no ideas left, and had forgotten the subject of his reflections. Then, hastily, he began to grope for at least one verbal concept, for the brain as a whole responds to the meaning of things, just as it does to one's own name, and, awakening from lethargy, renews its service with that lesson which it had temporarily denied us. However, this quest led to nothing either. It merely increased his vagueness. Only extraneous things pushed their way into his mind.

He suddenly recalled his spring encounter with Kovalenko. And again the falsely promised, non-existent story swam into his conviction as something complete and already composed, and he almost cried out when he realized that here, indeed, was a possible source of money – not the miraculous kind but the honest hundred or two – and, realizing all this and drawing the curtain of the middle window to shade the table, he sat down without

59

much reflection to write a letter to the editor. He success-fully negotiated the introduction and the initial polite phrases. What he would have done when it came to the substance was destined to remain an absolute mystery. For, at that moment, the same strange feeling alerted him. Now he had time to analyse it. The feeling was that of an engulf-ing emptiness, nostalgic and prolonged. The sensation had to do with the house. It declared the house uninhabited at that moment, that is, empty of any living thing except Serezha and his preoccupations. 'And Tornskjold?' he asked and then remembered that she had not been seen in the house since the previous evening. He noisily pushed his chair aside. Leaving open behind him the doors of the classroom and the nursery, and some other doors, he ran in to the vestibule. In the space beyond the sagging door leading into the yard, the white heat of five-o'clock-after-noon scorched like sand. Looking from above, it appeared to him even more mysterious and carnivorous.

*

'How careless of them!' he thought, passing from chamber to chamber (he did not know them all). 'All the windows open, and no one in the house or in the yard. The house could be entered and no one would say no. But why am I so vague? Anything might happen while I'm fumbling round.' He ran back, dashed down the stairs and ran out of the side door as if the house were on fire. And, as if in answer to a fire alarm, the doors of the servants' quarters banged in the depths of the yard.

'Yegor!' Serezha yelled in a voice not his own at the man who came running to meet him, a man who was chewing a last morsel and wiping his moustache and lips with the edge of an apron, 'tell me, I'd be greatly obliged, how can I find the Frenchwoman?' (he did not have the gumption to call her 'Frenchie' as the servants very precisely called the Danish woman and all her predecessors). 'Be quick, please, Margarita Ottonovna asked me this morning to give her a message and I've only just remembered.'

'The window over there!' The caretaker gruffly gulped as he hurriedly finished swallowing. Then, raising his arm and shaking his freed throat, he began chattering in a different vein as to how he could find the place, staring the while not straight at Serezha, but sideways at the neighbours' property.

It turned out that part of the humble three-storied building of undressed brick, which was joined at an angle to the mansion and which was rented from the Frestelns as a hostelry, had been set aside for the owners and was accessible from the ground floor of the mansion through a corridor skirting the nursery. In this narrow space, separated from the hostelry by a blind wall, there was just a room on each floor. The companion's window was located on the third floor. 'Where did all this happen before?' Serezha wondered as he tramped along the sloping boards of the corridor joining the two buildings. He was on the point of remembering, but refrained from probing further because, at that very moment, he came upon a spiral staircase hanging in front of him like an iron snail. Embracing him in its twist, it arrested his rush and made him take breath. But his heart was still beating fast when, spiralling to the end, it brought him straight to Arild's door. Serezha knocked without getting an answer. He pushed the door rather violently, and it crashed against the inner wall without evoking a protest. This sound, more eloquently than anything else, told Serezha that there was nobody in the room. He sighed, turned and, bending, gripped the spiral rail, but, remembering the door he had left open, returned to shut it. The door had swung open to the right, and that was where the handle was, but Serezha instead threw a furtive glance to the left and was dumbfounded.

There, on a knitted bedcover, her high heels pointing straight at the intruder, in a smooth black skirt which had settled athwart the bed festive and stiff like a corpse, Mrs Arild lay flat on her back. Her hair seemed black; her face was bloodless. 'Anna, what is it?' Serezha burst out and choked on the flood of air which carried this exclamation.

He threw himself toward the bed and dropped on his knees before her. With one hand he raised Arild's head and, with the other, began feverishly and awkwardly to grope for her pulse. He pressed the icy sinews of her wrist this way and that without finding the pulse . . . 'Lord, O Lord!' sounded in his ears and chest louder than the beat of horses' hooves whilst, staring at the dazzling pallor of her heavy eyelids, he seemed to be falling somewhere impetuously and endlessly, pulled down by the dead weight of her head. He was choking and on the point of fainting himself. But suddenly she recovered consciousness.

'*You, friend?*' she muttered vaguely, opening her eyes.

The gift of speech was restored not only to human beings. Everything in the room began to talk. The room was filled with noise as though full of children. The first thing Serezha did was to jump from the floor and shut the door. 'Ah, ah!' he said, foolishly repeating these monosyllables as he aimlessly tramped the room, now rushing toward the window, now toward the dressing-table. Although the room, which gave north, swam in lilac shadows, one could clearly distinguish the labels of the medicines in any corner, and there was not the slightest need, while searching among the phials and bottles, to carry each one separately to the window light. He did it only to give an outlet to his joy, which required a noisy expression. Arild had already regained full consciousness, and she now obeyed his injunctions only to please him. To please him, she consented to smell the smelling-salts, and the sharpness of the ammonia penetrated her as immediately as it would any normal person: her tear-stained face wrinkled with surprise, her eyebrows arched at an angle, and she pushed away Serezha's hand with the energy of one fully recovered. He also made her take some Valerian drops. As she drained the water, her teeth knocked against the brim of the glass, and she gasped as children do when they express their fully satisfied need.

'Well, what about our mutual acquaintances? Have they returned or are they still away?' she inquired, setting the glass on the table and licking her lips; and then, propping the pillow to sit up more comfortably, she asked what time it was.

'I don't know,' Serezha replied. 'It's probably near five.'

'The clock's on the dressing-table. Look, please,' she said, adding in a tone of surprise, 'I don't understand what you are staring at. You can't miss the clock. Ah – that photograph is Arild. The year before he died.'

'A wonderful forehead.'

'Yes, isn't that so?'

'And what a fine man! What an astonishing face. It's ten to five.'

'And now please give me the plaid – there it is, on the trunk . . . Thank you, thank you, that's fine. . . . I'd better lie for a while.'

Serezha, with an effort, pushed the resisting window, and it suddenly swung open. As if it were a bell that had been struck, the room momentarily rocked with spaciousness. The heavy scent of yellow dandelions, the grassy, resinous smell of red road-barriers from the boulevards filled the room. The screech of martins darted in disorder to the ceiling.

'Here, put this on your forehead,' Serezha suggested, handing Arild a towel soaked in eau de cologne. . . . 'Well, how do you feel now?'

'Oh wonderful. Can't you see?'

He suddenly felt that he would not have the strength to leave her. And therefore he said:

'I'll go in a moment. But you can't stay like this. You might have another attack. You should unbutton your neck and loosen your dress. Can you manage that yourself? There is no one else in the house.'

'*You'll not dare . . .*'

'You misunderstand me. There is no one I can send to you. I said, didn't I, that I would go,' he interrupted quietly and, dropping his head, slowly and awkwardly walked to the door.

She called him on the threshold. He looked back. Propping herself on one elbow, she was holding out her other hand. He approached the foot of the bed.

'*Come near, I did not wish to offend you.*'

He went round the bed and sat down on the floor with his feet under him. His pose promised a long and unconstrained chat. But he was so excited, he could not utter a word. And there was nothing to talk about. He was happy not to be under the spiral staircase, but close to her without having to take leave of her at once. She was about to break the oppressive and slightly comic silence. Then he quickly got on his knees, pressed his crossed hands against the edge of the featherbed, and let his head fall upon them. His shoulder blades began to move evenly and rhythmically, as though grinding something. He was either crying or laughing, but that was still not clear.

'What is it, what is it! I did not expect that. Stop, aren't you ashamed!' she kept repeating rapidly when his noiseless gasps turned into unrestrained sobs.

However (and she knew this) her words of comfort only encouraged his tears and, stroking his head, she connived at new floods of them. He did not restrain himself. Resistance would only have led to a stoppage, but there was a large accumulated charge which he wanted to release as quickly as possible. Oh, how glad he was that all those Sokolniki and Tverskoy-Yamskoys, and all the days and nights of the last two weeks had not stood their ground, but had started moving at last and travelling! He wept as though it was they, and not he, who were being torn. And they really were being whirled away, like logs on a swollen river. He wept as if expecting some purgation from the storm, which had suddenly burst as from a cloud, from all his worries about the millions. It was as though he expected these tears to influence the further course of his daily life.

Suddenly he raised his head. She saw his face, washed by a mist and, as it were, carried by it into the distance. In a state of some command, like a guardian over himself, he uttered several words, but they were wrapped in the same frowning and remote mist.

'Anna,' he said quietly, 'do not be hasty in your refusal, I implore. I ask your hand. I know it's not the way to say this, but how can I express myself better? Be my wife,' he went on even more quietly and firmly, quivering inwardly from the unbearable freshness in which this word was bathed, that he had just used for the first time in his life and that was as large as life itself.

And pausing for a moment to control the smile, which he had scooped up from some particular depth, he frowned and added even more quietly and firmly than before:

'Only don't laugh, I beg you. That would lower you.'

He stood up and walked aside. Arild quickly sat up, her feet dangling from the bed. She was inwardly in such a turmoil that, though it was all in order, her dress appeared crumpled and her hair unkempt.

'My dear, my dear, how can you!' she kept saying, trying at each word to rise, but forgetting to do so, and, at each word, spreading her arms in surprise like a guilty person. 'You've gone mad. You have no pity. I was unconscious. I can barely move my eyelids – do you hear what I am saying? I am trying to move them, I am not just blinking, do you understand that? And suddenly to ask me such a question, so bluntly! And don't laugh either. Ah, how you agitate me!' she exclaimed in another tone, as though in parenthesis or to herself, and, finding her feet, she quickly ran with this exclamation, as with a burden, to the dressing-table, behind which he stood sullenly listening to her, his elbow against the wood, his chin on the palm of his hand.

Gripping with both hands the edge, her whole body expressive of portentous conclusions, she continued to speak, splashing him with the light of a gradually mastered agitation:

'I expected this, it was in the air. I cannot answer you. The answer is in yourself. Perhaps, this will come true one day. And how I would like it to be so! Because . . . because I am not indifferent to you. You, of course, guessed that? No? Is that true? Tell me – didn't you really? How strange. But it's all the same. Well, anyhow, I want you to know it.' She faltered and paused for a moment. 'But I have been observing you all the time. There is something wrong with you. And do you know, now, at this very moment, there is more of it in you than the situation warrants. Ah, my dear, one does not propose like this. It's not just a matter of convention. But enough of that. Listen, answer me one question sincerely as you would your sister. Tell me: is there any shame on your conscience? Oh don't be frightened, for God's sake! Doesn't an unfulfilled promise or a neglected duty leave its mark? But, of course, of course, I assumed it myself. All this is so unlike you. You need not answer – I know: nothing that is unworthy of a human being can be part of you for long . . . . But,' she drawled thoughtfully, sketching something indefinitely empty in the air with her hand, while her voice sounded weary and hoarse, 'but there are things larger than us. Tell me, don't you have something like that inside you? That is a frightening thing in life. It would scare me like a strange presence.'

Though she did not stop talking at once, she added nothing more substantial. The yard was empty as before, and the adjacent buildings looked devoid of life. As before, the martins swept over them. The end of the day flamed like a mythical battle. The martins drifted forward like a cloud of slowly quivering arrows and then, suddenly reversing their sharp heads, rushed back, screeching. Everything was as before. But the room had grown a trifle darker.

Serezha was silent because he was uncertain of being able to control his voice if he broke the silence. At every attempt to speak, his chin drooped and trembled. He was ashamed to weep alone for his own private reasons, without being able to blame it on the Moscow countryside. His silence caused Anna extreme anguish. She was even more dissatisfied with herself. The important thing was that she agreed to everything; but she had failed to make it obvious by her words.

Everything seemed to be slipping unpleasantly through her hands and the fault was hers. As always on such occasions, she thought of herself as a soulless doll and, blaming herself, was ashamed to indulge in the cold rhetoric that her answers were supposed to contain. In order to correct this imaginary sin, and convinced that everything would now take a different turn, she said in a voice that echoed the whole of that evening, that is, in a voice that had developed an affinity with Serezha's:

'I don't know whether you understood me. I replied by agreeing with you. I am prepared to wait as long as necessary. But, first of all, you must put yourself in order – your own order, of which I know so little, and which you probably know only too well. I don't know what I am saying. Those hints spring up against my will. To guess them or surmise them is your business. Then there is this also: waiting will not be easy for me. But enough of this now or we shall wear each other out. And now listen. If you care for me even half as much. . . . Oh, please don't. What is it? I beg of you, don't, or you will destroy everything. . . . Well, thank you.'

'You wanted to say something,' he reminded her quietly.

'Yes, of course, I haven't forgotten. I wanted to ask you to go downstairs. Yes, really, listen to me. Go to your room, wash your face, take a walk. You must calm yourself. You don't think so? Well, all right then. Then let me ask you another favour, my poor dear. Go to your room all the same and do wash yourself. You can't appear in public with such a face. Then wait for me; I'll call for you and we'll go for a walk together. And stop shaking your head. It upsets me to look at you. It's pure self-suggestion. Say something, try – you must trust me.'

*

Again the emptiness of the sloping corridor-floorboards rumbled beneath him, and again he remembered the Institute courtyard. Again the thoughts evoked by remembrance rushed on in a feverish mechanical series which had no connexion with him. He found himself again in the sun-flooded room, which was too spacious and which therefore produced the impression of being uninhabited. In his absence, the light had shifted. The curtain of the middle window no longer shaded the table. It was the same light, yellow and slanting, which pursued its active play high in the air round the corner, and would then probably drop thickening violet shadows on her bed and the dressing-table stacked with phials. In Serezha's presence, the deepening lilac tones in Arild's room still knew some measure and behaved nobly enough, but how they would speed up without him, and how autocratically and triumphantly, profiting by his departure, the martins would assault her. He still had time to avert this violation and to catch up with the vanishing past; it was not too late to begin all over again and bring it to a different conclusion; it was all still possible, but very soon it would not be feasible. Why had he heeded her and left her alone? 'All right. Let us suppose,' he responded at the same time, out of that heated Anna series, to other feverish-mechanical thoughts that, unconnectedly, rushed past him. He pulled open the middle-half curtain and drew the end one, which made the light shift and bury the table in shadow so that now, instead of the table, the neighbouring room became flooded in light down to the far wall; this was the room through which Anna would be coming. The door of it was wide open. In his preoccupation, he had forgotten to wash his face.

'Well, and Maria. Well and supposing. Maria has no need of anyone. Maria is immortal. Maria is not a woman.' He was standing with his back to the table, leaning against the edge with his arms crossed. In his mind's eye, with revolting automatism, flashed the empty Institute premises, echoing steps, the unforgotten situations of the previous summer, and Maria's uncollected bags. The loaded baskets flashed before him like abstract concepts, and the suitcases with their straps and strings could have served as premisses for a syllogism. He suffered from these cold images as from a hurricane of idle spirituality, as from a flood of enlightened meaninglessness. Bending his head and crossing his arms, he waited for Anna in a state of irritation and longing, ready to rush to her and seek refuge from this nasty surge of obsessions.

'Well, congratulations to the failure. Thanks and the same to you. While you were trifling and trifling, another got away with it, leaving no trace. Well, God be with him. I don't know him, and I don't want to know him. What if there's no news and no trace. Well, supposing it is like that. Well, that's just fine.'

While he was bandying prickly comments with his past, the ends of his jacket slid to and fro on a sheet of writing-paper, the upper part of which had been scribbled on, but two-thirds of which were blank. He was aware of this, but the letter to Kovalenko also belonged to that extraneous series against which he was tilting.

Suddenly, for the first time in the past year, he realized that he himself had helped Ilyina to clear the apartment and depart abroad. Baltz was a scoundrel (he called him that inwardly). Then at once he felt certain that he had guessed right. His heart contracted. He was cut to the quick, not so much by the rivalry of last year as by the fact that, in Anna's hour, he could still be interested in something which had no connexion with Anna and which had acquired an inadmissible and, for her, offensive vitality. But, as abruptly, he realized that outside interference might also threaten him this summer unless he became more collected and positive.

He came to some decision and, turning on his heels,

scrutinized the room and the table as if seeing them for the first time. The strips of sunset budded with sap and gathered their final crimson. In a couple of places the air had been sawn in two, and glowing shavings fell from the ceiling to the floor. The far end of the room seemed plunged in gloom. Serezha placed a packet of writing-paper near at hand, and then switched on the electric light. While thus preoccupied, he had completely forgotten that he was meant to take a stroll with Anna.

'I intend to marry,' he wrote to Kovalenko, 'and am in desperate need of money. The story which I told you about, I am now rewriting as a play. . . . The play will be in verse.'

And he began to expound the plot of the story.

'Once upon a time, in the real conditions of our present Russian life, but which are so depicted as to give them a wider significance, in the milieu of the leading men of affairs of one of the capitals, a rumour is born, grows, and is enriched by all sorts of detail. It is transmitted orally without being checked in the newspapers because it is an illegal matter and in accordance with the recently revised legal code, it has become a criminal matter. It would seem that a man has come on the scene – a man eager to sell himself as a chattel at an auction to the highest bidder – and that the significance and profit of this transaction would become apparent at the auction. There seems to be an element of Wilde in this, or something having to do with women – and the unconfirmed buzz makes the rounds among the young merchants of the sort who model the furnishings of their houses on stage designs and who load their conversation with terms culled from Hindu spiritual lore. On the appointed day – for the news of the place and the day of the sale had incredibly reached everyone's ears – everyone leaves town, even though afraid of having been made a laughing stock. But curiosity wins and, besides, it is June, and the weather is simply wonderful. It all takes place in a country residence: the house is new, and no one has ever been there before. There is a crowd of people, all of the same set: heirs to big fortunes, philosophers, music-lovers, collectors, judicious amateurs. Rows of chairs, a platform with a grand piano, its lid propped open, and a small table nearby with a mallet on it. Several three-sectioned windows. At last the man appears. . . . He is still very young. Naturally, there is some difficulty over the name and, indeed, how can one name a man who is aspiring to become a symbol? However, there is a variety of symbols and, since a name must be found for him, let us for the time being label him algebraically – Mr Y, let us say. It immediately becomes apparent that there will be no fireworks, no circus smell, no Cagliostro, nothing of *The Egyptian* (even) *Nights*, and that the man was born in earnest and not without a purpose. It is evidently no joke; the gathering will be exposed to something within their common experience, without digressions into fictions, and they will not be able to get out of it. And therefore, with all the simplicity of prose, Mr Y is greeted with applause. He announces that whoever makes the largest offer for him will acquire the power of life and death over him. That he will take twenty-four hours to dispose of his gain as he has planned, leaving nothing for himself, after which he will begin his complete and incontestable bondage, the duration of which he now enstrusts into the hands of his future

73

master; for the latter will not only have the power to use him as he wishes, but also to kill him if it so pleases him. He has prepared, he says, a spurious note about his suicide, which will whitewash the murderer in advance. He is also ready to draw up, when required, any further document intended to cover with his good will anything that may happen to him. "And now," Mr Y declares, "I shall play and read to you. I shall play something unforeseen, that is impromptu; but the reading will be from a prepared text of my own." Then a new person walks across the platform and sits down at the table. It is a friend of Mr Y's. As distinct from his other friends who have bidden him farewell that morning, this particular friend, at Y's request, has remained at his side. This friend loves him no less than his other friends, but, as distinct from them, he does not lose his composure because he does not believe in the realization of Y's whim. He is an officer of the Treasury and a very thorough and reliable man. So Y has let him act as auctioneer during this transaction, to which he, the last remaining friend, attaches no value. He has remained to help him realize the whim, in whose accomplishment he does not believe, and then, in conclusion, to toast his friend on a long journey according to all the rules of auctioneering art. Then it begins to rain. . . .'

'Then it begins to rain,' Serezha scribbled on the edge of the eighth page and then transferred his writing from letter paper to quarto. It was a first draft of the kind a man writes only once or twice in a lifetime, taking all night at a sitting. Such drafts inevitably abound in water as an element, foreordained by its very nature to incarnate unvaried and persistently powerful movements. Nothing except the most general idea, unformulated as yet, and devoid of vital detail, settles in the writing of such initial evening outbursts; and the only remarkable feature of such writing is the natural way in which the idea is born out of the circumstances of experience.

The rain was the first detail in the sketch to stop Serezha. He transferred this detail from an octavo to a quarto-sized sheet, and began to amend and erase in an attempt to arrive at the desired lucidity. In places, he penned words that did not exist in the language. He allowed them to stay temporarily on the paper in the hope that they might, later, guide him through more immediate torrents of rainwater into that sort of colloquial speech, which originated from the intercourse of enthusiasm and usage. He believed that these runnels, recognized and accepted by all, would flow into his memory; and their anticipation dimmed his eyes with tears as if he wore a pair of incorrectly fitted spectacles.

If he had not been sitting, like every writer, at an angle to the table, with his back to both the entrances into the room, or if he had turned his head for the moment to the right, he would have died from fright. Anna stood in the doorway. She vanished, but not at once. Retiring a step or two from the threshold, she lingered in sight and close proximity just as long as she judged it necessary to preserve a balance between faith and superstition. She did not wish to tempt fate either by deliberate delay or blind haste. She was dressed in her outdoor clothes. In her hand she held a tightly furled umbrella because, in the interval, she had not severed her connexion with the outside world and had a window in her room. Moreover, when she was about to descend to see Serezha, she very sensibly glanced at the barometer, which indicated stormy weather. Forming like a cloud behind Serezha's back, and although dressed in black, she glittered whitely and smokily in a sunset beam of dazzling intensity, which shot out beneath the grey and lilac storm cloud that pressed down on the neighbouring garden. The torrents of light dissolved Anna as well as the parquet floor, which curled corrosively beneath her like vapour. From two or three movements made by Serezha, Anna, as in the Game of Kings,* guessed both his trouble and its lifelong incorrigibility. After seeing him move the cushion of his fist across his eye, she turned away, gathered her skirt and, crouching as she walked, in a few long and powerful strides tiptoed out of the classroom. Once in the corridor, she increased her pace a little and dropped her skirt, and this she did while still biting her lips and as noiselessly as before.

To refuse him had involved no labour. Everything happened by itself. The window of her room was already occupied to its full width by the shifting sky. From its purple layers it was clear that she would never arrive undrenched even at the nearest corner. Anna now felt that she must all the more urgently undertake something to escape remaining alone with her fresh and rapidly suppurating nostalgia. The mere notion of being left alone all night in her room made her turn icy with horror. What would become of her if this actually happened? Running through the yard into the street, she hired a cab with its hood already raised. She drove to Chernyshevsky street, where an English friend of hers lived, hoping that the storm

*A card game in which the winner has the right to ride round the room astride the losers.

would continue to rage and make it impossible for her to return home, and that her friend would be obliged to put her up for the night.

'. . . So it begins to rain outside the house,' Serezha scribbled. 'And this is what takes place in front of the windows. The ancient birch trees set their leaves free in whole swarms and wave them a ceremonious farewell from the hillock. In the meantime, fresh flurries of leaves, becoming entangled in their hair, whirl away and thin out in white gusts. Having waved them on and lost them from sight, the birches swing toward the cottage. Darkness falls, and, just before the first clap of thunder peals, Mr Y begins to play on the grand piano inside.

'For his theme, Mr Y picks the nocturnal sky as it looks when it emerges from the bath-house, clad in the kashmir down of clouds, in the vitriol-and-incense vapour of the wind-blown forest, with a strong rush of stars washed clean to their last chink and looking larger. The glitter of these drops, which can never be detached from space, however much they may try to break away, is already strung above the grand-piano thicket. Now, running his fingers along the keyboard, Mr Y abandons and then resumes the theme, surrenders it to oblivion and imposes it on the memory. The window-panes are flattened torrents of mercurial chill; with armfuls of enormous air, the birch trees move before the windows; and scatter it everywhere, showering it onto the shaggy waterfalls, while the music weighs out bows to right and left, and keeps promising us something from the road.

'And what is so extraordinary, every time anyone attempts to doubt the honesty of the statement, the player

77

splashes the doubter with some unexpected miracle of sound. It is the miracle of his own voice, that is, the miracle of their tomorrow's way of feeling and remembering. The force of this miracle is such that, jokingly, it can cleave the basin of the piano and, at the same instant, crush the bones of the trading class and the Vienna chairs; and yet it scatters fast silver speech and sounds all the quieter, the more frequently and rapidly it is repeated.

'He reads in exactly the same way. He expresses himself thus: "I shall read you so many passages of blank verse, so many columns of rhymed quatrains". And again, each time anyone thinks it does not much matter, which way these carpet fictions fall – head or feet South or North of the Pole, then descriptions and similes of prodigious magnetic sensitivity manifest themselves. Those are images, miracles of the word, that is, examples of complete and arrowlike submission to the earth. That is the direction which their future morality, their bent for truth, will follow tomorrow.

'But how strangely this man appears to experience all this. It is as if someone kept showing him the earth and then hiding it in his sleeve, and he interpreted living beauty as a limiting distinction between existence and non-existence. His novelty consists in this, that he has grasped and raised to a constant poetic symptom this contrast, which is conceivable only for an instant. But where can he have seen these appearances and disappearances? Is it not the voice of mankind that has told him of an earth ever flitting in a succession of generations?

'All this is, fully and without cuts, true art; from the whispering frontiers, it talks of infinities; everything is born of the richest, bottomlessly sincere, terrestrial poverty. He intersperses his reading with playing: he hears the rustle of French phrases; and he is enveloped in scent. In low tones, he is requested to forget about everything else and to continue only the piece he is performing and not to interrupt it – but this is not what he wanted.

'Then he rises and addresses them, saying that their love touched him, but they did not love him enough. Otherwise, they would have remembered that they were at an auction and why he had brought them together. He says that he cannot reveal his plans to them, for they would intervene again as they had done so many times, and suggest another solution and another form of help, possibly even a more generous one, but necessarily incomplete and not of the kind his heart had prompted. That he has no current value in that large issue in which man has been printed. That he must make himself a commodity of exchange, and they must help him in this. They may think his project a lamentable fantasy. Very well. But they must either hear him entirely or not at all. If they hear him, then let them blindly submit to him. He resumes his playing and reading; in the intervals, numerals crackle, and work is found for his friend's idle hands and throat; and then, after twenty minutes of mad fever and in the very heat of glycerine hoarseness, on the ultimate crest of unparalleled perspiration, he falls to the lot of one of the most sincere seekers, a person of the strictest principles, and a renowned philanthropist. But it is not at once, not that very evening, that this man allows him the taste of freedom. . . .'

5

NEEDLESS to say, this is not an original of Serezha's draft. He himself did not complete it. There was much on his mind that was never recorded on paper. He was just pondering a scene of city riots when Mrs Fresteln, drenched to the skin and furious, burst into the room, dragging after her the reluctant Harry, who was evidently abashed at the prospect of the imminent scandal.

Serezha had assumed in his plot that, on the third day, let us say, after the transaction, a conversation of major importance and perspicuity would take place between the philanthropist and his chattel. He had conceived that, having lodged Mr Y separately and having exhausted him by over-luxurious treatment, and himself – by worry, the rich patron could no longer bear the anxiety and would call on Mr Y with the request that, since he did not know how to employ him more worthily, he depart to the four corners of the world. This Mr Y would refuse to do. On the night of this conversation news would be brought to the country of the riots which had just occurred in the city and which had begun with acts of violence in the very neighbourhood where Mr Y had scattered his millions. This news would discourage both of them: Mr Y in particular because, in the acts of violence that had gained such wide notoriety, he would detect a return to the past, whereas he had hoped for an enigmatic renewal, that is, a complete and irreversible renaissance. And then he would depart. . . .

'No, it's unbelievable. I almost broke my umbrella! Mrs Fresteln exclaimed. *'je l'admets à l'égard des domestiques,' mais qu'en ai-je à penser si....* But, heavens, what's the matter with you? Are you ill? I'm a fine one! Wait just a minute. Harry, you must go to bed immediately, immediately! Varya, you will rub him down with vodka, and we'll talk tomorrow. There's no point in sniffling now, you should have thought of it before. Go now, Harry dear. The heels, that's important, the heels, and also rub his chest with turpentine. Tomorrow there will be nice words for all of you; for you and for Lavrenty Nikitich, but Mrs Arild will be the first to give an account of herself.'

'What's she done?' Serezha asked.

'At last! I didn't want to mention it in their presence. I didn't notice anything at first. Don't be angry. Are you having any trouble? Anything to do with the family?'

'Excuse me all the same, but how has the Missis displeased you?'

'What Missis? I don't understand anything. You're blushing! Aha, so that's it! So, so. Well, all right. Yes that's it – regarding my maid. She hasn't been home since the morning. She left the premises with the rest of the servants. But the others at least thought better of it in the evening....'

'And Mrs Arild?'

'But that's not decent. How do I know where Mrs Arild is spending the night? *Suis-je sa confidante?* Now this is why I have stopped in here, my dear Sergey Osipovich. I'd ask you, my dear, to see to it that Harry packs his games and school books tomorrow morning. Let him pack them himself as best he can. Of course you will afterwards rearrange everything without letting on that it was part of your plan. I feel you want to ask me about the linen and the other things? Varya is responsible for all that and it does not concern you. I believe that, where possible, children should be given the illusion of a certain independence. Here even appearances stimulate beneficial habits. In addition, I should like you, in the future, to devote more attention to him. In your place, I'd lower the lamp a little. Allow me! Well, just like this, don't you think? Isn't it really better than the way you had it? But I'm afraid of catching cold. We leave the day after tomorrow. Good night!'

*

One day, in the early days of his acquaintance with Arild, Serezha began discussing Moscow with her and checking her knowledge of that city. Besides the Kremlin, which she had sufficiently examined, she named a few other sections inhabited by her acquaintances. Of those names he now remembered only two: the Sadovaya-Kudrinskaya and Chernyshevsky streets. Discarding the forgotten directions, as though Anna's choice were as limited as his memory, he was now ready to guarantee that Anna was spending the night at Sadovaya. He was convinced of this, because that meant complete frustration. To find her at this hour in such a large street, without the faintest notion where or in whose apartment to seek her, was impossible. Chernyshevsky street was another matter, but it was certain that she could not be there because of the way his hopeless longing, like a dog, ran ahead of him on the pavement and, struggling to escape, dragged him after it. He would have certainly found her in Chernyshevsky street if only he could have imagined that the living Anna, of her own free will, was indeed in that place where it was merely his desire (and what strong desire!) to situate her. Convinced of failure, he hurried to test with his own eyes this non-destined possibility, because he was in a state when the heart would rather gnaw the hard core of hopelessness than remain inactive.

It was full morning, overcast and chilly. The nocturnal rain had just ceased. At each step the sparkle of the silver-hued poplar trees kindled above the almost black grey of the drenched granite. The dark sky was sprinkled with their whitish leaves as with milk. Their felled leaves speckled the pavement like soiled scraps of torn receipts. It seemed as if the storm before departing, had imposed upon these trees the duty of examining the after-effects, and left in their fresh grey hands the whole of that tangled morning so full of surprises.

On Sundays Anna used to attend the service in the Anglican church. Serezha recalled her telling him that one of her acquaintances lived somewhere in the vicinity. Accordingly, full of his preoccupations, he placed himself right opposite the church.

He stared vacantly at the open windows of the dormant vicarage, and his heart gulpingly picked on morsels of the scene, greedily gobbling the damp bricks of the buildings and the moist foliage of the trees. His anxious glances likewise crunched the air which, avoiding his lungs, passed drily into some other unknown region of his body.

In order not to attract anyone's suspicion, Serezha periodically strolled down the full length of the street. Two sounds only disturbed its drowsy quiet: Serezha's footsteps and the throb of some machine in the vicinity.

That was the rotary press in the printing works of *The Russian Word*. Serezha felt all bruised inside: he was breathless for the wealth which he had to absorb, but was hardly able to do.

The force, which had infinitely expanded his sensation, was the absolutely literal nature of his passion, namely, that quality of it, thanks to which the tongue seethes in images, metaphors and, even more, in enigmatic forms that escape analysis. Needless to say, the whole street with its unbroken gloom had become wholly and roundly identical with Anna. Here Serezha was not alone, and he knew that. And who, in truth, has not experienced this! However, the feeling was more spacious and precise, and here ended any assistance from friends or predecessors. He saw how painful and difficult it was for Anna to be the city morning, how much the superhuman worth of nature cost her. She gloried silently in his presence and did not appeal for his aid. Dying with longing for the real Arild, for all this splendour in its briefest and most precious abstraction, he watched how, swathed in poplars as in ice-packed towels, she was sucked into the clouds and slowly threw back her brick Gothic towers. This brick of purplish non-Russian baking looked imported, and for some reason from Scotland.

A man in an overcoat and soft felt hat emerged from the newspaper office. Without turning his head, he walked in the direction of Nikitskaya. Not to arouse his suspicion if he should glance back, Serezha crossed from the newspaper pavement to the Scottish one and strode in the direction of the Tverskaya. Some twenty paces from the church he saw Arild inside a small room. At that very moment she had come to the window. When they had recovered from the shock, they began to talk in hushed tones as if in the presence of sleeping people. This they did because of Anna's friend. Serezha stood in the middle of the pavement. It seemed they were talking in whispers so as not to rouse the city.

'I heard someone walking up and down the street for a long time, someone who could not sleep,' Anna told him. 'And then I suddenly thought it might be you! Why didn't you come near the house at once?'

*

The carriage corridor tossed from side to side. It looked endless. The passengers were asleep behind the ranks of lacquered, firmly shut doors. Resilient springs deadened the rumbling of the carriage. It resembled a luxuriously beaten-up, cast-iron featherbed.

The edges of the featherbed fluttered most pleasantly and, reminiscent somehow of paschal egg-rolling, a rotund chief-conductor rolled down the corridor in boots and wide breeches, a round cap on his head and a whistle dangling from a strap. He perspired in his winter uniform and, to comfort himself on the way, adjusted his strict pince-nez. It surprised one by its minuteness amid the large beads of sweat that dotted his whole face and made it resemble a slice of Swiss cheese. If he had happened to observe Serezha's pose in a carriage of a different class, he would have surely nudged him or, in some other manner, roused him from oblivion. Serezha was drowsing with his elbows against the edge of the lowered window. He drowsed and then woke, yawned, admired the landscape, and rubbed his eyes. He put his head out of the window and bawled melodies which Arild had once played, but no one heard his bellowing. Whenever the train came out of a curve into the straight, a graceful immobile current of air imposed itself upon the corridor. Having run and panted their fill, the wild doors of the end platforms and the toilets spread their wings and, to the roar of increasing speed, it was wonderful to feel that one was not merely witnessing a flight but was oneself one of the straining birds, with Schumann's bravura in one's soul.

It was not the heat alone that had driven him out of his compartment. He felt uncomfortable in the company of the Frestelns. It required a week or two more for their impaired relations to become normal again. He blamed Margarita Ottonovna least of all for their deterioration. He admitted that, even if he were her adopted son and she owed him some leniency and indulgence, there was some cause for her despair during the recent commotion before their departure.

After her last nocturnal reprimand, it had pleased him to absent himself the whole day on the very eve of the departure, knowing full well what a hullaballoo would reign in the household early next morning.

'The blinds!' someone would unexpectedly squeal and Yegor would miraculously materialize himself, like a living person, out of pieces of matting. 'The blinds! Why didn't you! . . . '

'What about the blinds?'

'What's that, you fool! Are they to stay here, do you think?'

'Will anything happen to them?'

'And did you beat the dust out of them?'

86

'May the rain drench you, Lavrenty. Leave me alone!'
'Varya, my dear, this is not an outing, you know.'

*

'. . . But, in the end, the devil take her, that Arild. He is
to be pitied, of course: a worthless intriguing woman, but
what was to be done once the scythe had struck stone. But,
if it has come to that, it is a different argument altogether;
and there was a human way of doing everything. He had
seen her off on the 5.45 train from the Bryansk station –
well, and that was that! And he could have managed it so
that not a soul at home would have needed to know where
he had been or what he had lost. On the contrary, everyone
would think: there's a real man, a decent self-respecting
man. But that was obviously old-fashioned; everything
now was different. He had to shut himself off, you see,
from the leave-taking and he's not embarrassed at their
hours-long scrutiny at their curiosity to see whether he's
. . . adapting himself and getting accustomed. Well, what's
one to do? Dismiss him? . . . Don't bother, lady, that's
not the way. I'll tuck it in myself, but. . . . Oh, the devil
take it, it's rotten stuff! The second one to break. I told you
to use a rope, didn't I? But how dismiss him when there
was so much confusion all round and when it was absolutely clear from what had happened that his salary was
not just for fun. But then, if you please, a job was no joke
either and one must value it. In his justification, it might be
said that a new decadent expression had been coined – "to
experience". However, to experience or to expose one's
secrets to external scrutiny could probably be done in a
human way, whereas in his case, the morning after one is

face to face with an absolutely unrecognizable and unsuitable man, a very Christ of passivity: if it were seriously proposed, he would drive nails into a box with his head; but, alas, a household requires anything but that, and such is not the function of a tutor in a decent family. . . . And now they were travelling and he with them. Why was he with them? But how dismiss him?

'In Tula they missed their connexion just as the train pulled in at the station and, with horror, they saw their connexion train running off at an angle in the direction of Kaluga. That night was horrible. . . . But they were rewarded for their ten-hour torment. About an hour ago a long distance express came by through Tula, and they were now installed in it more comfortably than they could have been in their local night train. Anton Karlovich and Harry were sleeping, but they, poor wretches, would have to be wakened in twenty minutes.'

The chief conductor found the carriage to his liking, for he kept reappearing. The landscape was really astonishing. For example, look at it this very moment when, frozen at full speed, the noisy, dirty train floated and seemed to repose upon a spaciously spread arch of sheer and blazing sand, while opposite the embankment, far beyond the flood meadows, a large and curly estate seemed to float at rest upon a barely quivering hillock. When less than fifteen miles remained, one might have thought this was already Roukhlovo: the white gleams of the manor house and the railings of the park, crumpled by the indentations of the hill, on which it seemed to have been placed like a necklace that had been unclasped – all this seemed to be an exact copy of what he had been told. The park contained many silver poplar trees. 'Dear ones!' Serezha whispered and, closing his eyes, exposed his hair to the gallop of the on-coming wind.

*

So this was why men had need of the word 'happiness'. Although they had merely talked, and he had merely shared her worries and had helped her to prepare for the journey . . . although they would experience another, more complete proximity . . . yet they would never be closer than they had been during those unforgettable ten hours. Everything in the world had been understood; nothing more was left to grasp. All that remained was to live, that is, to chop understanding with one's hands and to wallow in it; all that remained was to please it, just as it had pleased them – what was spread out all round them with railways lining its face and terms. What happiness!

But how lucky that she had spoken of her family! How easily this might not have happened. Wretches! a lot they understood about what debases or ennobles a family tree. But another time of her unfortunate father (a remarkable case!). Serezha now understood where she had acquired her wide knowledge, which made her seem twice as old and ten times more austere. That was all inherited. It explained her calm mastery of it all. She had no need to be amazed at herself or to seek a loud name for her gifts. Before her marriage she had had it anyway, and it was a very well-known one.

Her ancestors were of Scottish descent. Mary Stuart had been mentioned in this connexion. And now it was impossible not to feel that this name in particular had been missing all that morning in the overcast Chernyshevsky street.

But, at last, the strict chief-conductor nudged the deafened passenger and warned him and his fellow-travellers that they must descend at the next stop.

This way the way, then, people had moved from place to place that last summer when life still appeared to pay heed to individuals, and when it was easier and more natural to love than to hate.

*

Serezha stretched himself, fidgeted and began to yawn uncontrollably. Suddenly this stopped. Alertly he raised himself on his elbow and glanced about him soberly and rapidly. The reflection of a street-lamp splashed the floor. 'Winter,' he thought at once, 'and this is my first dream at Natasha's in Ousolie.' Fortunately, no one had observed his very animal awakening. And – ah ! – there was something else he must not forget. He had dreamt of something formless and, whatever it was, it still made his headache. More remarkable still, this nonsense had a name while he saw it. 'Lemokh', it was called. But what did that mean? One thing was certain : he must get up. His appetite was wolfish, and he hoped that he had not overslept the guests.

In a minute he was already drowning in his brother-in-law's frieze embraces, which smelled strongly of iodoform. The latter still held a tin-opener in his fist when he rushed to greet Serezha with his arm fully extended. This, together with the hearing-aid protruding from his pocket like tangibly materialized sincerity, somewhat spoiled the sweetness of their embrace. And the opening of the tins could not

90

be renewed with the previous expertise and went lame. Questions, abrupt and artificially unrefined, showered across the tins. Serezha stood there, feeling glad and puzzled why one should play the fool when one could be a natural fool without trying. They did not like each other.

On the table stood a neat row of vigorous, freshly awakened vodka glasses. And a complex assortment of wind and percussion snacks made the eyes beam. Above them, conductor-like towered black bottles of wine, ready at any moment to crash out and wave on a deafening overture to the accompaniment of all kinds of laughter and puns. The spectacle was all the more impressive because the sale of wine had been prohibited throughout Russia, but the factory evidently lived as an autonomous Republic.

It was already late, and the children could only be seen in bed.

The whole room seemed to swim in brandy. Whether it was the effect of light or the furniture, the floor appeared to have been polished not with wax, but rosin, and his slithering feet felt beneath them not the waxed-over splinters, but glued and, as it were, stained hair. All things with facets and any play of light were flooded by the hot yellow of the furnishings ('Karelian birch tree, what are you thinking?' Kalyazin sang lyingly for some reason), as with lemon cordial. Serezha too possessed this quality. He thought that the piercingly lighted house should appear to the bearish blue-white night as a minute brazier full of tiny coals, glowing among the snowdrifts.

'Aha, there's a real frost! I'm glad!' he exclaimed, standing behind the fold of a curtain and staring into the darkness.

'H'm ... yes, it's freezing hard,' the brother-in-law grunted, wiping his sauce-ambered fingers with a handkerchief.

'I haven't any boots with me. I forgot to bring them or, rather, to buy them.'

'That can be put right. You can get them here. But what are we talking about, pray? So to speak, man is here, so to speak. ... Have some Nelma. Siberian fish. And Maksun. Have you heard of them, brother? No? Well, I knew you'd never heard of them.'

Serezha grew more and more light-hearted, and it is difficult to tell what he might not have done. But a vague confused trampling of feet made itself heard in the corridor. There people were taking off their coats. Soon there came into the dining-room, all flushed from the frost, Natasha and a girl Serezha did not know, and also a dry, definite and very alert man, whom Serezha rushed to meet ahead of Kalyazin and whom he greeted effusively, joyfully and almost apprehensively. Then all the gaiety dropped away from him. In the first place, he knew this man and, besides, he was confronting something tall and alien that devalued Serezha from head to foot. It was the personification of the masculine spirit of fact, the most modest and the most terrible of spirits.

'And how's your brother?' Serezha began in confusion and then stopped.

'He's still alive,' Lemokh replied. 'He was wounded in the foot. He's convalescing with me. I'll probably be able to fix him up at home. Glad to see you. And how are you, Pavel Pavlovich?'

'Just imagine,' Serezha mumbled even more distractedly,

'he may have concealed it for military reasons, but not one of us realized it was the mobilization. Everyone thought it was the manoeuvres. I'm sorry but I don't know what they call those training tactics. Anyhow, we all thought it was merely routine exercise. But they were already being transported to the front. In a word, I saw him in July two summers ago. And just think, their detachment was going by in barges and they were moored for the night near the estate where I was employed as tutor. That was two days before war was declared. We only put two and two together afterwards. Do you understand?'

'Yes, I know about your conversation with my brother. He told me about it.'

But what Serezha would not admit was that he had again failed to ask Lemokh his name the night they met.